ROBIN HOOD

PRISONS, PARTIES & POWERBOATS

ROBERT MUCHAMORE'S
ROBIN HOOD

PRISONS, PARTIES & POWERBOATS

HOT
KEY
BOOKS

First published in Great Britain in 2023 by
HOT KEY BOOKS
4th Floor, Victoria House, Bloomsbury Square
London WC1B 4DA
Owned by Bonnier Books
Sveavägen 56, Stockholm, Sweden
bonnierbooks.co.uk/HotKeyBooks

A CIP catalogue record for this book is available from the British Library.

ISBN: 978-1-4714-1334-6
Also available as an ebook and in audio

1

Typeset by DataConnection Ltd
Printed and bound in Great Britain by Clays Ltd, Elcograf S.p.A.

Hot Key Books is an imprint of Bonnier Books UK
bonnierbooks.co.uk

ROBIN HOOD

THE STORY SO FAR . . .

Once upon a time, **Robin Hood** lived with his dad, **Ardagh**, and half-brother, **Little John**. He was a regular kid, spending his days battling boredom in school and free time practising archery stunts or hanging with his bestie, **Alan Adale**.

Everything changed when Robin's dad got sent to prison for a crime he didn't commit.

Robin's half-brother Little John discovered that his mum was the super wealthy **Marjorie, Sheriff of Nottingham**, and went to live with her, while local gangster **Guy Gisborne** put a bounty on Robin's head, forcing him to hide out in Sherwood Forest and join a gang of rebels led by **Emma** and **Will Scarlock**.

With his new rebel pals, Robin blew up cash machines, hacked computers, caused a massive flood, flipped a police car, paint-bombed a house and became a social media sensation, with footage of his escapades getting millions of views.

AND NOW . . .

It's springtime in Sherwood. After a brutal winter, Will Scarlock's rebels are gaining strength, with more members, organised security teams, and steady supplies of food and equipment to their base inside the abandoned Sherwood Castle Resort and Casino.

Things look good for Robin too, reunited with his friend Alan Adale and chilling in the castle penthouse with girlfriend **Josie Longshanks**.

Meanwhile, Robin's dad Ardagh is freshly released from prison and running a popular campaign to beat Guy Gisborne and get elected as the next Sheriff of Nottingham.

But life for our thirteen-year-old hero isn't perfect. Guy Gisborne has upped the bounty on Robin's head to one million pounds, while his friend Marion Maid is locked up in Pelican Island prison, where she faces daily violence and bullying.

Worst of all, national elections are less than six weeks away. Despite numerous scandals, Nottingham's outgoing sheriff, Marjorie Kovacevic, still has a narrow lead in the race to become president. And she's promised to wipe out Robin and the rebels if she wins.

1. 99,000 BROWN BALLOONS

The Rolls-Royce SUV was humongous, but Little John still seemed too big for it as he squeezed out of the rear door. Photographers snapped pictures as his girlfriend Clare Gisborne exited the opposite side, while their bodyguard scooped armfuls of shopping from the boot.

'Clare!' a journalist shouted as the pair set off across carpeted marble towards the revolving door of Capital City's third-poshest hotel. 'How do you feel about claims that your father is responsible for the deaths of three workers at Mile End landfill site?'

'Is Guy Gisborne fit to be the next Sheriff of Nottingham?' another added.

Clare's eyes flickered resentment, but her mouth stayed shut. As Little John put his arm around his girlfriend, the media turned on him.

'John Hood, will you be supporting your father's bid to become Sheriff of Nottingham or your mother's bid to become president?'

John tutted. 'I'm neutral. Can't you lot think of a new question?'

As Clare whispered, 'Just say nothing' in John's ear, a TV reporter noticed the bodyguard holding bags with swag from the kind of shops where the cheapest item is a £200 baseball cap.

'How much did you spend?' the TV guy asked.

'Would your brother, Robin, approve of your shopping spree?' another asked. 'While refugees in Sherwood Forest go hungry?'

As John and Clare neared the revolving doors, a photographer stepped into their path and fired a powerful camera flash in their faces. It was noon and sunny, so the flash was just to annoy them. If either seventeen-year-old reacted, it would be all over the news:

SON OF PRESIDENTIAL CANDIDATE GOES ON RAMPAGE AFTER EXTRAVAGANT SHOPPING SPREE

John would have loved to use his hundred-and-twenty-kilo frame to splat the photographer but was smart enough to avoid the trap.

A bellboy opened a gold-framed entrance next to the hotel's revolving doors. John, Clare and their bodyguard hurried inside, as two security guards blocked off the media. Clare felt the tension in her boyfriend's arm as she surveyed the hotel lobby and breathed scent from massive bouquets of fresh flowers.

'You OK?' she asked.

'One day . . .' John said, then pounded a fist into his palm.

Clare smiled. 'You knock 'em down and I'll boot 'em in the soft parts.'

John stepped through a velvet rope barrier opened by a volunteer in a red *VOTE MARJORIE* T-shirt.

A deserted marble hallway took them to the outer lobby of the hotel's conference centre. The ceiling was hung with banners bearing the People's Party logo and a list of Sheriff Marjorie Kovacevic's campaign promises:

```
SLASH IMMIGRATION
TAKE BACK CONTROL OF OUR COUNTRY
A FAIR DEAL FOR TAXPAYERS
TOUGH ON REBELS
TOUGH ON CRIME
```

The far side of the lobby was mad chattering chaos, as a hundred journalists and influencers queued to be admitted to the conference hall.

They were here for a staged event at which Sheriff Marjorie planned to announce a radical new healthcare plan for the nation. But her staff were having a nightmare because the computers that checked guest IDs and printed entry badges kept crashing.

There were also problems with ear-piercing feedback from the building's PA system and the giant screens along the ramp leading into the five-hundred-seat auditorium. These were supposed to set the mood, with images of Sheriff Marjorie shaking hands with doctors and listening to hospital patients, but the screens kept glitching and showing daytime TV.

John spotted his mum's campaign manager, Tina. He had to wait before speaking, because she was ripping into a delivery driver holding a battered tablet computer.

'We're supposed to have six thousand pre-inflated *red* balloons,' Tina spat. 'You're telling me you've brought ninety-nine thousand brown balloons?'

'There are seven truckloads out back,' the driver said. 'It's what your office ordered.'

Tina gasped, then screamed, 'Who would order seven truckloads of brown—'

'Can't wait all day, love,' the driver interrupted, tapping the tablet screen with a stylus. 'I have other customers.'

'I am not your *love*!' Tina blasted. 'Stick your balloons. I have a million other things to deal with.' She spun away, showing the driver their conversation was over. Then she had another gasping meltdown when she noticed her boss's son and his girlfriend in front of her.

'What? Why? Hello!' Tina blurted. 'You're not scheduled here this morning.'

'Half-term,' John explained. 'Mum said her announcement would take an hour and that we could fly back to Nottingham in her chopper.'

'Right,' Tina said, then opened her arms to the surrounding chaos. 'Well, you can see it's all gone wrong. Your mother's healthcare announcement is running *very* late.'

'Where's Mum at?' John asked. 'I'll say hello and let her know we're here.'

Tina winced. 'Your mother just threw a hot cafetière at an intern. If I were you, I'd steer clear.'

'I know that mood,' John said warily, then glanced around wondering where to go. 'So?'

Tina pointed towards the **NO ENTRY** sign with carpeted steps beyond it. 'Upstairs, double doors on the right. There's a campaign team buffet sitting there getting cold. Grab a bite and I'll see you up there. If your mother doesn't sack me first.'

2. VALUABLE WORK EXPERIENCE

Marion Maid was four hours into a six-hour shift. Her body was slick with sweat and trapped inside a plastic overall that went from her head to her white rubber boots. One of the few good things about being a prisoner was free healthcare, and she wore a foam leg brace following surgery to straighten her crooked right leg.

The brace itched as she walked along a shiny metal gantry. Below were two giant food mixers, like you'd find in any kitchen, except the bowls were bigger than a car and the mixing paddles were the size of doors.

Pelican Island prison's meat processing plant had a central control room, and each mixing job arrived with detailed instructions on a touchscreen. First, Marion sterilised the vast mixer by turning a valve and releasing a blast of superheated steam.

While the steam hissed and swirled, she read the ingredient list and gathered items from racks of metal shelves behind: four twenty-kilo bags of salt, thirty kilos of celery powder, twelve litres of autolysed yeast extract, two large tubs of mustard powder and a bucket of sodium erythorbate.

The prison restricted inmates' access to blades, so Marion had a frustrating job opening each hefty bag by lifting it up and catching it on a wall-mounted hook. As the steam from the mixer's sterilisation cycle wafted away, she began emptying sacks and tins over the edge of the gantry into the vast bowl.

Next came the gross bit. While Marion worked on preservatives and seasonings, male inmates on the upper level had prepared one and a half tonnes of animal products. The mixture varied for each batch, from minced pork for posh sausages to the gruesome fat and mechanically recovered sludge that went into bargain burgers.

When Marion hit the **MIXTURE READY** button on the touchscreen, a giant overhead chute opened and meat, fat, and glossy foaming blood splattered from above. She reached up with a long metal oar to knock down a slab of mince that had stuck in the chute, then turned on the mixing paddle. Slow to begin, then adding speed as three huge blocks of fat turned to paste.

'How's my best girl today?' a prisoner named Paul shouted down the chute.

'I'll live.' Marion sighed as she looked up the metal chute at Paul's blood-smeared boots and overall.

'Are you feeling educated?' Paul asked.

Marion smiled behind her plastic visor. 'My brain gets bigger by the minute,' she said dourly.

This was a joke, because young offenders like Marion were supposed to get an education. But Pelican Island was run for profit and King Corporation's management had decided that teenagers could be educated with thirty hours a week of work experience.

'You off shift soon?' Paul asked, as he grabbed a handle to close the chute and start on the next batch.

'Not soon enough.' She blinked sweat out of her eyes and occasionally used the oar to push down blobs of meat that stuck to the side of the shiny bowl. When the mix had an even colour and no lumps, she pushed a button to retract the paddle, then switched on a pump.

The mixer sounded like a giant farting vacuum cleaner as the meat paste got sucked down a pipe to an adjoining room, where prisoners turned it into burgers, sausages, hot dogs and meatballs.

The most physical part of the job came next: going down into the bowl and blasting all the meaty gunk off with a ferociously hot steam wand. But it took a while for all the mix to get sucked out. Although Marion's workstation didn't have a chair, she'd made one by stacking salt bags in a gap between shelves.

Workers were only supposed to drink during hourly breaks, so Marion glanced about furtively before flipping up her visor and downing half a litre of tepid water from a rinsed-out paprika tin.

She shut her eyes, but before getting any rest she heard boots squeaking on the steps up to the gantry. She feared getting told off for slacking by Kerry the floor supervisor, but as Marion stumbled to her feet she realised it was far worse.

3. CHILLI SQUID GAMES

Little John swung through the double doors into a banqueting suite, taking in a space with bay windows overlooking the hotel's rose garden. An elaborate buffet had been set out on a table that ran the room's full length.

'Giant shrimp and caviar,' Clare said keenly.

'Decent spread,' John agreed, as a hotel waiter looked up guiltily from his phone and scuttled out through a service door.

John skewered a shrimp as big as his thumb and headed for the chocolate fountain.

'You're such a child!' Clare laughed as John ran the shrimp under molten chocolate and popped it in his mouth.

'Vile,' John admitted, grinning and coughing as he took a napkin to wipe chocolate off his chin stubble.

As John lifted a plate off a stack, Clare felt her phone vibrate. The screen indicated a video call from her mate Amber, but she got a shock when she answered.

'Wassup, Gisborne!' Robin Hood said cockily. 'Long time no speak-o!'

'How are you showing as Amber?' Clare spluttered as John looked at the screen over her shoulder. 'Did you hack me?'

'Amber's account was in a data breach a few months back,' Robin explained. 'Tell her to change her password.'

'You destroyed my parents' house and *terrified* my little brothers,' Clare growled. 'I'm so not talking to you.'

'Don't hang up!' Robin begged. 'I have to tell Little John something urgent, but he's not answering.'

John patted the pockets of his tracksuit and looked worried. 'I had my phone in the car . . .'

Clare tutted as she passed him her phone.

'Chat soon, Clare-pops,' Robin teased cheerfully. 'Kissy kiss!'

'You're a creepy worm,' Clare shouted.

'Thanks for winding up my girlfriend,' Little John said, scowling at Robin as he took the phone. 'What's so urgent?'

Instead of answering, Robin started howling with laughter. 'What is that tracksuit you're wearing?'

'It's Matt Holland boutique,' John answered. 'Probably cost more than your entire wardrobe.'

'Looks like someone ate a load of carrots then puked down your front.'

'Get to the point,' John sighed. 'Clare's furious, and now you're annoying me.'

'I wasn't expecting you to rock up at your mum's press briefing,' Robin said. 'I need to tell you something in private, away from Clare.'

John glanced around the room, looking for cameras. 'Are you stalking us?' he asked.

'Don't speak to him,' Clare urged, then looked angrier as John turned to face one of the bay windows so she couldn't hear.

Robin grunted. 'You think I'd bother stalking you, bruv? First, you're not that important. Second, if I logged in and saw you and Clare doing it, I'd be scarred for life.'

'What's this about?' John asked, speaking quietly, aware that Clare was steaming because he'd not ended the call.

'Don't eat chilli squid from the buffet,' Robin said.

John had an epiphany as he glanced around and spotted a large bowl of chilli squid on the buffet table. 'Are you behind the chaos downstairs?'

'The rebels' finest work,' Robin answered proudly, then launched into an explanation without being asked for one. 'Sheriff Marjorie was hot favourite to become president, but scandals and screw-ups have squeezed her opinion poll lead to almost zero. She hired a new public relations company to stop the rot, but they have *terrible* cybersecurity. My hacking skills are just average, but it only took minutes to breach their server and access *every* document, phone and email.'

John nodded, while warily eyeing Clare's scowl and folded arms. 'So that's why the computers can't print name badges, screens are showing episodes of *Property Hunt*, and there are seven truckloads of brown balloons?'

'The balloons!' Robin laughed. 'I forgot about them. I'd *love* to be a fly on the wall when Marjorie finds out she's spent a hundred grand on poo emoji balloons!'

John sounded curious. 'How do you know I'm not gonna walk downstairs and tell my mum what you've done?'

'You tell everyone you're not taking sides,' Robin answered. 'If you grass me up to your mum, you'll be crossing that line. Besides, the damage is done – her people must know they've been hacked by now.'

'You're a clever little dickhead,' John admitted. 'And *fine*, I won't tell Mum. But what's this about the squid?'

'I had no idea you'd be at the conference,' Robin said. 'But apparently chilli squid is your ma's favourite.'

'She always orders squid in restaurants,' John agreed.

'We have an insider in the hotel kitchen,' Robin explained. 'Anyone who eats that squid will be spending a week on the toilet, instead of the campaign trail.'

'That's nasty,' John snapped. 'She is my mum, you know.'

Robin turned angry. 'If *your* mum becomes president, she's promised to jail me for life and use the army to blast every rebel and immigrant out of Sherwood Forest. I'd have put something deadlier than salmonella in her squid. But Will Scarlock says the rebels won't win by sinking to Marjorie's level and committing murder.'

John groaned with frustration. 'So I'm supposed to stand in a room while my mum and her campaign staff eat poison?'

'I risked everything to warn you when you walked into the buffet,' Robin told his brother. 'I didn't want you getting sick, but go snitch if you like. At least if you do, we'll *finally* know whose side you're on.'

4. MICROWAVE MACARONI

Uma and Sarika were seventeen-year-old twins, doing life for murdering their foster parents and Geography teacher. They were way bigger than Marion and part of a gang called Mafia 13 that had it in for her.

'You can't come up here,' Marion said, eying the twins' heavy butchers' aprons and meat-spattered rubber boots. 'If the floor supervisor comes . . .'

'Do we look scared?' Uma said, then tutted with contempt.

The twins worked on a different part of the floor, chopping slabs of frozen cow with a band saw and dropping them into mincers.

'You gonna get me some microwave macaroni, Marion?' Sarika asked.

'Marion Maid's Microwave Macaroni,' Uma sang weirdly, enjoying the Ms and the look of fear behind Marion's visor.

'Can't run on that messed-up leg of yours,' Sarika snarled, as she swished a little fat-smeared filleting knife in Marion's face. 'Give me your blue card.'

'Blue card!' Uma parroted.

'It's in my locker,' Marion said as she backed into the shelving racks, scared but trying not to show it.

Each prisoner had a blue payment card. If friends or family sent money, the card could be used for phone calls, overpriced snacks or personal items from the prison shop.

'We know Auntie put thirty bucks in your account,' Uma said, as her sister tapped the blade against Marion's plastic face visor. 'Buy us four macaronis when the shop opens and we can be friends.'

Marion didn't want to get stabbed, but if she gave in to the twins they'd keep asking for more stuff – and still beat her up when the money ran out.

'I've stashed a chocolate bar that my dad sent,' Marion said hopefully, pointing up to a high shelf. 'Raisin and cookie dough.'

The twins looked at each other. Sarika pulled back the knife.

'Get it then,' Sarika hissed. 'Chop chop.'

'But we still want macaroni,' Uma added. 'Original cheddar, not filthy chicken and broccoli flavour.'

There was a step stool to reach higher shelves, but Marion ignored that and used the metal shelves like a ladder. Fuelled by fear, she pulled up her legs and rolled to the back of a shelf three metres up before the twins realised they'd been suckered.

'Down!' Sarika demanded, as she jumped too late to grab Marion's trailing boot.

As the factory's metal extractor fans whooshed near her head, Marion crawled quickly along the shiny metal shelves, batting down bags of corn starch and onion powder to clear a path.

'I'll break you,' Uma roared, ducking the flying produce as she chased Marion at gantry level.

'It's a dead end,' Sarika added. 'Where you going, tiny girl?'

With life sentences, Uma and Sarika had nothing to lose. Marion reckoned she had one chance to save herself from getting cut, but it wouldn't be easy.

She jumped down where the racking met the wall. Her rubber boots landed noisily on the gantry and she fought the pain that shot up her bad leg as she snatched a steam wand attached to a long rubber hose.

Sarika turned when she realised what was about to happen, but not fast enough. Marion pulled a trigger and aimed the hose. Thee-hundred-degree steam shot down a rubber pipe and out through a jet nozzle. Sarika's visor saved her face, but the intense blast melted her plastic overall and scorched her back and shoulder.

As Sarika collapsed in a wailing heap, Uma picked up a sack of salt and came at Marion using the sack as a shield. There was a visor over her face and thick butcher's gloves covering her hands, so Marion went for the salt bag and melted the plastic.

The fifty kilos of salt broke free, and Uma stumbled into her flailing sister. While the twins screamed and got tangled, Marion stepped forward with the steam wand and blasted them all over.

Uma's melted overall looked like strings of cheese as she pulled herself up, using the railing at the edge of the gantry. Marion's visor was badly fogged as she closed in with the wand, but rather than risk more pain, Uma dived over the gantry into the mixer. Her head hit the shiny metal bowl with a cartoonish thud, then she thrashed about, slathered in dark pink meat sludge, as the vacuum snagged the remains of her overall in the outlet pipe.

Sarika grabbed Marion's rubber boot as she tried to escape, so Marion left it behind. As she stumbled along the gantry in one sock and one boot, a guard in the plant's control room finally saw that something was wrong and hit the alarm.

When prisoners hear an alarm, they're supposed to drop to the ground and place both hands behind their heads. But Marion was halfway down the steep metal steps that led off the gantry, and more worried about Sarika coming after her with the knife.

As Marion reached the last step, a dark figure emerged on her blind side. She tried to drop, but the prison guard sent her sprawling by jamming an electrified stun stick between her shoulder blades.

'Down, scum!' the guard roared.

Marion crashed to the floor. Her visor flew off as she skidded across the polished concrete into a storage cabinet. She gasped for air as she rolled onto her back and held up her hands, but the guard still stomped on Marion's socked foot and delivered three more zaps with the stun stick.

5. FURTHER TECHNICAL ISSUES

Sheriff Marjorie Kovacevic peeked between curtains at the side of a small stage. TV crews and photographers stood up front. Journalists in rows of seats behind stared at their phones, bored. Since her healthcare announcement was two hours late a few had already left.

'I know it's been a stressful morning,' campaign manager Tina whispered to Marjorie as a stagehand fitted the candidate's lapel microphone. 'Keep it light and stay on message.'

Marjorie scowled at Tina, then switched on a smile as she walked on stage. The intro music was meant to be the upbeat opening bars of her specially composed campaign theme song 'Vote for a Brighter Tomorrow', but instead the auditorium speakers blasted out a funeral march.

'Some technical gremlins today,' Marjorie told the crowd weakly.

Instead of Marjorie's words, the gathering heard a deafening blast of guitar feedback, bird squawks, fart noises and metal dustbin lids banging together.

At the same time, the screen behind the presidential candidate switched from a People's Party logo to a photo of Robin Hood, aiming his bow and wearing a T-shirt with *Catch Me If You Can!* printed across the front.

Photographers snapped and TV crews recorded as Marjorie stared gormlessly at her lapel microphone and turned an angry red. Then speakers and lighting died as Marjorie's stage manager decided it was better to kill the power than risk more embarrassment.

As the press stumbled about in the greenish light cast by emergency exit signs, they sensed that the routine candidate's healthcare briefing had become a major story about Robin Hood and rebel sabotage. The area in front of the stage got tangled with limbs, backpacks and smartphone voice recorders as the reporters yelled questions.

'Sheriff Marjorie, will you catch Robin Hood?'

'Is it true your campaign team bought seven truckloads of poop emoji balloons?'

'How can you be president when your team can't even organise a press briefing?'

'What would you do to Robin Hood if you could get hold of him right now?'

Marjorie looked like a grenade with the pin pulled, glaring into space as two security guards shuffled her off stage.

'Thank you for your patience,' Tina told the media. 'Miss Kovacevic has been advised to leave. Certain systems have been compromised and we cannot guarantee everyone's safety. Please leave the auditorium. No further questions.'

Marjorie howled as she stormed through fire doors into a tatty backstage hallway. 'How could this happen?' she shouted. 'He's a child!'

'Rebel operations are increasingly sophisticated,' one security guy said, as Tina caught up with her boss.

'We'll debrief in the banqueting suite,' Tina said breathlessly. 'Everyone upstairs and out of sight before the press find us.'

Little John and Clare tried to be invisible in one of the banqueting suite's bay windows as Marjorie almost ripped the double entry doors off their hinges

'We'll minimise damage,' Tina soothed, as she tailed her boss. 'I'll offer one-on-one interviews. I'll issue a statement reminding everyone that Robin Hood is an attention-seeker and terrorist, wanted for a number of serious crimes. Then I'll—'

She was cut off as Marjorie grabbed the base of the chocolate fountain and sent it hurtling across the table.

'Why am I surrounded by idiots?' Marjorie roared, as molten chocolate splattered over ceilings, carpets and the rest of the food. 'How can our systems get hacked like this? I want McKenzie from security *now*!'

'McKenzie's busy working out what happened with the guest registration,' Tina said gently.

'We know what happened,' Marjorie shouted, as chocolate poured off the buffet table. 'Robin Hood happened – and my lead in the presidential race went down the toilet.'

'Let's calm down,' Tina suggested. 'We've survived worse.'

Marjorie eyed a waiter who'd stepped into the room after hearing the chocolate fountain crash. 'Boy, get me a glass with ice and a full bottle of whisky,' she shouted. 'Something old. Whatever it costs.'

As Marjorie slumped heavily in a dining chair, she sighed, then pointed at the chilli squid. 'Tina, pass that over.'

John eyed the poisoned squid anxiously as Tina picked it up. He knew Marjorie wasn't a good person, but confusingly she was also his mum. He didn't love her the way he loved Robin and his dad, but he didn't hate her either.

'I need to eat,' Marjorie said. Tina gave her the squid bowl and the waiter came back with a silver tray, holding a crystal tumbler and a dusty whisky bottle.

'This is thirty-five-year-old Glencherub at two thousand a bottle,' the waiter began. 'Would you like to taste?'

'Just brim my glass,' Marjorie ordered as she spiked three squid rings with a fork. 'Then give us privacy.'

As the waiter set the tray down and poured whisky, a sprightly woman entered in a daffodil yellow dress and matching heels.

Little John considered yelling 'Don't eat the squid!' but Robin was surely watching via the hotel's hacked CCTV. Plus, if he said something now his mum would be furious that he hadn't told her about the rebel sabotage immediately.

'McKenzie,' Marjorie said to the woman in the yellow dress, as the waiter handed her a big tumbler full of whisky. 'What does my highly paid online security guru have to say for herself?'

McKenzie rubbed sweat off her brow. 'It seems the rebels hacked the main server at our new public relations firm,' she began.

Marjorie knocked back half of the whisky, then dropped the fork back into the squid bowl. 'Isn't it your job to check them out?'

McKenzie squirmed. 'The agency told us they had robust systems, but it seems they weren't updating their security software. Which means it's useless.'

'Useless, like a lot of things around here,' Marjorie carped.

McKenzie seemed shaken, but relieved that she hadn't been fired already. 'Miss Kovacevic,' she continued nervously. 'Given what happened in the auditorium, it's reasonable to believe this hotel's security cameras and video conferencing system have also been hacked.'

Marjorie's gaze shot about, seeking cameras. 'You mean Robin Hood and the rest of the rebel dirtbags are watching and listening right now?'

'It's likely,' McKenzie agreed, as Tina's jaw dropped.

'They saw me curse, trash a chocolate fountain and order two thousand bucks' worth of whisky?'

'I've asked the hotel manager to shut down cameras by physically unplugging them,' McKenzie said. 'But I still think we should leave the building.'

Marjorie drained the rest of her whisky and set the empty glass down hard on the marble buffet table. 'Tina, call my pilot. I want my helicopter up in fifteen minutes.'

'It might be better to stay in Capital City,' Tina urged. 'I can get you on news and talk shows. If you fly back to Nottingham, it will look like you're running scared.'

'Pilot,' Marjorie repeated, as she stood up holding the squid bowl that had been on her lap. 'I've heard enough of your advice today.'

Tina stepped backwards as her boss loomed over her. 'With respect, Marjorie, I really think you're wrong to fly back to – AAAAARGH!'

The campaign manager dived sideways, but not fast enough to avoid the bowl of chilli squid that Marjorie hurled at her head.

'Do as I say, Tina,' Marjorie blasted, before taking the whisky bottle, then looking at John and Clare, huddled together in the bay window. 'Come on, you two, we're flying home.'

As Tina sobbed and Marjorie stormed out, Little John studied the squid rings spilled over the floor. He'd watched the whole time and his mum hadn't eaten a bite.

6. SNITCHES GET STITCHES

The fingers locked behind Marion's head were numb as she knelt down, facing the crust of frost on the wall of a huge meat locker. She didn't dare look around when the room's insulated door swung open, because that was all the excuse one of the meaner guards would need to take another swipe at her.

'Quite a mess out there,' Kerry, the floor supervisor, said.

Marion sighed with relief. Her boss was strict, but wouldn't kick you in the back or zap you with a stun stick like the guards.

'Uma and Sarika are heading to county hospital with serious burns,' Kerry explained. 'And your mixing machine is out of order until an engineer comes to replace the broken outlet pipe.'

Marion heard something bounce on the floor and turned her head enough to see the rubber boot Sarika yanked off when she ran away.

'Stand up, put your boot on,' Kerry said wearily.

Marion's whole body ached as she stood. Her fingers and toes were so numb that she struggled to get her foot back inside the boot. When she stumbled forward, Kerry grabbed her plastic overall to steady her.

'I realise this isn't your fault,' Kerry said, smiling behind her visor. 'Two older girls came to your section with a knife. I can fetch a form if you want to file a report.'

Marion shook her head as she tucked her hands under her armpits, trying to get some feeling back.

'You're a good worker and no trouble,' Kerry said. 'I can speak to the head guard and get you put into protective custody.'

Marion didn't answer.

Kerry tutted. 'Is it really worth protecting those two?'

'I've got enough enemies in here without getting labelled as a snitch,' Marion said sadly.

'Uma and Sarika have Mafia 13 tattoos. Their gangmates will be after you.'

'Can I go?'

Kerry sighed and gestured towards the meat locker's heavy door. 'I can't help if you won't speak up.'

The best thing about meat processing was that workers got a shower before and after every shift. And since Marion had been kept back after shift change, she had the rare privilege of a washroom to herself

She took time, spraying her boots with foaming blue disinfectant before putting them in the bottom of her locker, dumping her white overall in the sterilisation bin, then showering and rinsing out sweaty clothes.

The clothes trailed drips as she moved back to her locker. The only mirror was a scuffed sheet of polished metal, but it was reflective enough for Marion to look over her shoulder and see little burns where the stun stick fried her skin.

'Eight-four-seven-one, Maid!' A guard named Ruth shouted through the barred door, making Marion jump. 'You should have been ready ages ago.'

Ruth had worked at Pelican Island for decades without earning promotion. She wasn't the kind of guard who'd knock you around, but she moaned about everything and wouldn't lift a finger to help a troubled inmate.

'Sorry, boss,' Marion said, as she began dressing in a clean prison uniform.

The white socks and underwear always came with a disinfectant smell and a rainbow of stains from all the inmates that had worn them before. On top of underwear, inmates wore baggy nylon shorts that usually had cigarette burns and fluorescent orange T-shirts with **PELICAN ISLAND INMATE** written front and back.

If the clothes were grim, the footwear was worse. The plastic slides only came in two sizes and their loose fit and rigid soles were designed so that inmates couldn't move faster than a slow shuffle.

'Dry the floor before you leave,' Ruth ordered, as Marion's head emerged through a shirt with faded blood splatter and a ripped sleeve.

While Pelican Island's meat processing plant was modern, the bits of the prison that didn't make a profit for King Corporation got neglected.

As Ruth led Marion though double-locked gates and across the courtyard to the huge prison tower that inmates called Central, they got hit by a stench that was a mixture of damp, mould and corroded sewage pipes. It had been oozing into the fabric of the building for decades.

'Juvenile inmate coming through!' a bulky guard shouted, unlocking a metal gate and letting them into Central's main atrium.

7. LESS SCHOOL, MORE WEIGHTS

Robin had been given the morning off school to run the hack on Sheriff Marjorie's press briefing. Then he pushed his luck by skipping afternoon lessons and going for a sneaky workout in Sherwood Castle's first-floor gym.

His body ached as he sat astride a weight bench, doing bicep curls with 20 kg barbells, while sweat streaked his bare chest and Metallica exploded from his earbuds. After slotting the twenties back on the barbell rack, Robin decided he'd had enough.

He stared into a wall mirror as he ripped the Velcro to take off his lifting gloves. Robin was too fond of treats to ever get a proper six-pack, but he liked how muscly his chest and shoulders looked – and best of all, he'd finally had a growth spurt. Five centimetres in two months.

As Robin burrowed down his bag for his post-workout protein bar, someone switched on the row of giant TVs that hung on the back wall behind treadmills and cross-trainers.

The gym was always dead in the early afternoon, but when school kicked out it got invaded by a dozen lads and a handful of girls. The teens who came through the door in workout clothes were mostly three or four years older than Robin. They were always friendly, but Robin was too young to be part of their social group. And he was glad to get his workout in early, because they always hogged the best equipment.

Today was different, because the teens lined up in front of the big screens, catching up on news they'd missed while they'd been in lessons. Robin pulled one earbud out so he could hear the newsreader.

'. . . After leaving the conference centre there were yet more problems for the presidential candidate. When Miss Kovacevic's helicopter tried to take off from a nearby building, her pilot was refused permission because the helicopter's airworthiness certificate had expired.

'Sources close to the presidential campaign say this was another issue related to rebel hacking. After a delay of more than an hour, Marjorie Kovacevic and her entourage were forced to return to Nottingham by car . . .'

The TV screens showed a scowling Marjorie and Little John getting in the back of a giant Rolls-Royce. Then laughter erupted around the gym as the channel showed a CCTV clip that the rebels had released, where Marjorie destroyed the chocolate fountain.

'Robin's right here!' a beautiful sixteen-year-old Nigerian named Tiwa noticed, then told him, 'What you did today was brilliant!'

Tiwa pulled Robin into a hug and the difference in height meant his face got buried in her chest.

'I'm sweaty,' Robin warned, his words muffled as his cheeks went bright red.

'Sweat all you like,' Tiwa said, as she landed a giant kiss on Robin's forehead. 'No way Marjorie can stay ahead in the polls after this humiliation.'

Tiwa's looks and brains made her the popular kid who everyone copied, so Robin got engulfed. Three more girls kissed him. All the gym-rat boys lined up to give Robin slaps on the back, with macho phrases like, 'You the man' and, 'You ever need help, we got your back!'

A year earlier, Robin was a geek with one friend who nobody had ever heard of. Now cool seventeen-year-olds were *literally* lining up to tell him he was great, and it made him feel good.

'It wasn't just me,' Robin said, trying to be modest. 'Six people helped with the hacks and Emma Scarlock's down in Capital City, organising people on the ground.' He realised his moment of glory was up when the older kids picked up weights, started treadmills, and began gossiping about another kid who'd drunk two bottles of wine, fallen out of a castle window and been chased by a bear.

Robin dumped his protein bar wrapper in a bin and grabbed his bag, then cracked a big smile as he saw his best mate and girlfriend step through the gym lobby.

'Thought we'd find you here,' Josie said.

'Ditching afternoon lessons,' Alan added. 'Naughty boy.'

'And why does *my* boyfriend have lipstick on his forehead?' Josie asked.

Robin caught his reflection in a wall mirror and wiped his forehead on his sweaty gym towel.

'We thought we'd go to the pool,' Alan said. 'If you're not too tired after your workout.'

Robin wasn't keen, because loads of annoying little kids went to the pool after school. But he changed his mind when Josie added, 'It would be nice to actually see you. Apart from school, you've spent the last two weeks hiding in the Nest with your computers.'

Robin shrugged. 'Sorry I've not been around. But the result was worth it, right?'

Alan laughed and nodded. 'The fart sounds every time Marjorie tried to speak were hilarious.'

'And the chocolate fountain,' Josie added. 'I think Marjorie needs anger management.'

'No way we could have planned *that*,' Robin pointed out.

'I have missed your dopey face though,' Josie said, as she held her arms out for a hug.

'Missed you,' Robin said, hugging his girlfriend as Alan made a gagging noise. 'I'll grab my swim shorts and see you there.'

8. THE SUPER SEVEN

'Move fast and stay close to the wall,' Ruth told Marion as they crossed Central's hexagonal atrium.

There was a filthy glass dome overhead, and the shouts and screams of two thousand men in the cells above were like a football crowd from hell. The suicide nets wouldn't catch everything that inmates tossed from balconies, so Marion moved as fast as her rigid slip-on shoes allowed.

A couple of storeys up, Marion saw four officers in riot gear dragging an elderly inmate by his ankles. She didn't have much to feel lucky about, but daily trips through Central on her way to meat processing reminded her that some parts of Pelican Island were much nastier than where she lived.

A two-hundred-metre walk across an empty gravel exercise yard took Marion and Ruth to Stable Block. The name came from the building's original function, back when horses pulled goods from prison factories to the loading dock.

Accommodation for twenty-four horses had been converted into ten cells with three triple bunks in each. There was also a tiny windowless punishment cell, a toilet and shower area with a spectacular population of cockroaches, a dining room and a guards' office bristling with CCTV screens.

With capacity for ninety female inmates aged between twelve and eighteen, Stable Block went almost unnoticed in a prison housing five thousand adult men, nine hundred women and six hundred adolescent boys. It also had a four-hundred-bed hospital for the criminally insane.

But though Stable Block was regarded as the softest part of the prison, living there was still zero fun.

'Had to traipse to meat processing 'cos this one caused trouble,' Ruth complained to her senior colleague Danielle, as a heavy metal door squealed open to let them through Stable Block's main door. 'Put the kettle on, will you, pet?'

There were only ever two guards on duty in Stable Block, but older or smaller officers like Ruth were always paired with someone like Danielle, a woman the size of a small car whose favourite expression was 'Do what I say if you want to keep some teeth inside your head.'

At this time in the afternoon, Stable Block was on half-and-half. This meant prisoners were confined to the cell block, but weren't fully locked down and could use the showers or move between cells.

Marion's nine-bunk cell was to the right, furthest from the entrance. She'd hoped Ruth would walk her all the way there, but her elderly escort got distracted by an inmate asking for medication.

'Oh, look who!' a tattooed Mafia 13 member named Devon hissed when Marion passed the first pair of cells, either side of a hallway barely wide enough for two bodies to pass.

'Put our twins in hospital?' another shouted threateningly, clanking something against the rusty bars. 'We're gonna end you, Maid.'

Marion was thirteen, but most of the girls who got in trouble serious enough to end up in Stable Block were in their late teens.

She got more shouts and sparks from a flying cigarette butt from the next cell, then peered at mouldy tiles as she passed the shower block. Several of Mafia 13's baddest members were treating a new inmate to a cold shower and hard slaps.

This was bad for the newbie, but good for Marion, who had almost reached her cell before someone blocked her path. Guppy was a tattooed fifteen-year-old and more of a wannabe than an actual member of Mafia 13.

'So not scared of you,' Marion sneered, but still glanced behind, hoping Ruth could see. She walked into Guppy with enough force to make her stumble. But Guppy was heavier and shoved Marion into cell bars, then swung something heavy that she'd knotted in the arm of her prison-issue hoodie.

Marion ducked as the metal object hit the bars, sending a clang echoing down the corridor. As Guppy took another swing with her homemade cosh, the knot in the bottom broke and the floor was showered with bolts and washers Guppy had smuggled out of a prison factory.

Marion bobbed up and smashed her palm hard into Guppy's nose, then the reassuringly ominous figure of Marion's sixteen-year-old cousin Freya Tuck stepped out of the last cell on the right and sent Guppy flying with a kick in the back.

'Did her brain fall out?' Freya asked, as she looked at the bolts spilled over the floor.

A couple of Guppy's cellmates loomed as Freya pushed Marion behind her and blocked the hallway. As Marion glanced back, her cellmate Posh Sophie stepped out to back up Freya.

But before the standoff turned into something more, senior guard Danielle's voice came out of a ceiling speaker like the voice of God. 'There are no fights on my shift,' Danielle stated. 'Back to your cells, or I'll make you all sorry.'

The girls knew Danielle meant business, and backed into their cells.

'Not over, Maid,' Guppy hissed, blood dripping from her nose as she walked off.

Marion felt shaky and sick as she stepped into her cell and the almost reassuring stink of sweat and body spray. The cell's three triple bunks were packed tight and as the youngest inmate, Marion had to suffer the bottom bunk, next to the squat toilet that inmates used when cell doors were locked.

'Cheers,' Marion said warily, eyeing Freya and a couple of her other cellmates who gathered around her bunk. 'I couldn't help what happened in processing. The twins started on me.'

'The way I heard it, Uma and Sarika got what they deserved,' Freya said proudly. 'Better fight than get steamrollered.'

'But there's twenty Mafia 13 girls in this block.' Marion sighed. 'They'll all be after me.'

'Mafia 13 can kiss my hairy butt,' Freya said, making sure she said it loud enough for girls in other cells to hear. 'We're the Super Seven and nobody's gonna mess with us!'

9. MATT MAID IS VERY ANNOYING

Robin had muscle ache from working out and brain fuzz from late nights masterminding his latest hack, but the pool turned out to be a laugh, especially when Marion's eleven-year-old brother Matt and his mates started a battle with pool noodles and plastic balls from a ball pit.

Things ended badly for Matt when he made a sexist comment about Josie's bum. She chased to the shallow end, got Matt in a headlock and slapped his back so hard that he wound up with a massive red welt shaped like her hand.

Matt liked thinking of himself as a cool dude and leader of his little crew of skateboarders. He looked mortified as everyone laughed at him, while Josie got claps and high fives.

'I'm not a violent person,' Josie said as she waded back to Robin and Alan, who floated amidst the brightly coloured balls. 'But Matt is too much.'

'You should be violent more often,' Alan joked. 'You're really good at it.'

'I'm always hanging with you at the penthouse,' Josie said, as she looked warily at Robin. 'Matt's mums make me dinner and stuff. Will they be annoyed?'

Robin snorted. 'If Matt said that in front of Indio and Karma, they'd ground him for a month.'

More coloured balls zipped through the air as the excitement of Matt vs Josie subsided. But Robin was distracted when Marion's dad, Jake 'Cut-Throat' Maid, emerged from the changing area and strode purposefully along the poolside.

Cut-Throat wasn't dressed to swim. Kids froze in shock or ran into the water as the enormous biker approached, his boots trailing dirt. There were no official lifeguards, but parents of younger kids were on hand. One shouted, 'Excuse me,' while another mum stepped in front of Cut-Throat.

'You can't wear outdoor shoes poolside,' the mum said, planting hands on hips. 'Why are you here?'

'Need Robin Hood,' Cut-Throat said.

Robin was too far off to hear, but people pointed him out.

'What does he want?' Josie asked.

Robin shrugged. 'How should I know?'

'Well, don't go off with him,' Josie said irritably. 'I've barely seen you.'

'I know,' Robin agreed as he waded out of the pool and headed towards Cut-Throat.

'What's wrong with your phone?' Cut-Throat asked irritably when Robin got close.

Robin rolled his eyes. 'I don't carry it in the pool.'

'You did a nice job hacking Marjorie,' Cut-Throat said. 'I might have another use for your tech skills.'

'I was up at five preparing the hack.' Robin sighed. 'I'm knackered.'

'It's for Marion,' Cut-Throat said.

That changed everything, because Robin missed Marion and still felt guilty about her getting busted.

Cut-Throat backed up to some flip-out seats. His weight made the plastic bend like it was about to snap.

'I'd take the boots off,' Cut-Throat explained, as a mom mopped up boot prints and glowered. 'But my socks aren't great either.'

Marion's dad always intimidated Robin, even more so as he shivered in swim shorts.

'Remember when your dad was locked up in Pelican Island?' Cut-Throat continued. 'My biker pals looked after him. We smuggled in treats, and miniature phones so you could talk to him?'

'Sure,' Robin agreed. 'My dad would have been eaten alive if you hadn't helped.'

'We had a system for smuggling stuff onto Pelican Island using drones,' Cut-Throat explained, as three squealing girls ran past. 'Each drone could carry eight hundred grams of contraband. That's like a couple of mobile phones, or five packs of cigarettes, sweets or anything else an inmate might want.'

'How did the drones get in?'

'My mate Ollie has a houseboat on the lakefront. They'd pilot drones across Lake Victoria and land in the exercise yard near our people. Sometimes a drone crashed, or guards blasted one, but most got through.'

'Not any more?' Robin asked.

Cut-Throat shook his head. 'Every drone we've sent in the last month drops out of the sky as it nears Pelican Island. Ollie has used different flight paths and smaller drones, but nothing gets through.'

'Some kind of signal-blocking system,' Robin speculated.

'To make it worse, when our drones got blocked, a new smuggling network sprang up supplying inmates with everything we used to. Bikers dominated smuggling on Pelican Island. Now a gang called Mafia 13 runs the show.'

Robin nodded thoughtfully. 'How do they get stuff in?'

'Not certain,' Cut-Throat admitted. 'But before drones, the usual way to smuggle stuff onto Pelican Island was through corrupt guards.'

'How is this for Marion?' Robin asked suspiciously. 'You only let men into your gang, so there's no female bikers to stick up for her. I heard she's had a nightmare with bullies.'

Cut-Throat unnerved Robin with a growl. 'Whoever controls smuggling on Pelican Island can move stuff around and influence the whole prison,' Cut-Throat said irritably. 'If I wanted to get Marion a phone, medicine or a birthday treat, we could get it to her. But I can't get stuff to Marion if we can't get it to Pelican Island in the first place.'

'Fine,' Robin said. 'If it helps Marion, I guess I'm in.'

'Any ideas?' Cut-Throat asked.

'I'll need to research,' Robin began, before pausing to think. 'I tinkered around with a crashed police drone last summer. I know a bit about how drones work and how to knock them out of the sky. I'm also connected to a lot of good hackers. I'll try and find an expert.'

'Good man,' Cut-Throat said, as he squeezed Robin's shoulder, then stood up. 'I'll get Ollie to send details. Like the type of drones and routes we used.'

Robin nodded. 'Soon as I'm dressed, I'll head to the Nest and start work.'

As Cut-Throat exited, Robin jogged back to Alan and Josie. They'd joined a couple of classmates, sitting on the steps at the pool's shallow end.

'I've got to go look at something in the Nest,' Robin explained.

'Are you having a laugh?' Josie spat, as her eyebrows shot up. 'We're hanging out for the first time in ages.'

'One hour maximum,' Robin said. 'I'll be back at the penthouse before dinner.'

'Better be,' Josie warned, as she swept her hand across the water to splash Robin's legs. 'I won't be around if you're late.'

10. SHOT THOUGH THE HEART

Robin did most of his hacking from the Nest, which was a former surveillance room above Sherwood Castle's casino. His hair was still damp from the pool when he arrived in the skylit space, and by the time he'd settled at his screen he'd received a long email from Cut-Throat's pal Ollie.

The excitement of a new challenge made Robin forget aches and tiredness. The first stage of any hack or operation is to gather as much information as possible about your targets.

Once he'd read everything Ollie sent, Robin tried to find detailed maps of Pelican Island, skimmed a website that told the prison's history, and looked at companies that sold anti-drone systems. Their tech ranged from catapults that fired ball bearings and sticky foam to pricey military systems with radar and missiles.

Robin's most powerful hacking tool was the Super, a bright green supercomputer that used artificial intelligence to find patterns in vast amounts of information in its data lake. Its hard drives had terabytes of data stolen from police forces, banks, airlines and any other organisation slack enough to let their data get hacked.

The Super also linked to hundreds of live information sources, from CCTV cameras that Robin had set up around Sherwood Castle, to Locksley police radios and a live feed from Chinese spy satellites.

Robin started a bunch of search queries, looking for information about Pelican Island's security, the Mafia 13 prison gang, and personal information on the island's inmates and staff.

The Super rarely completed a search of its data lake in less than fifteen minutes, and might take days if you used an advanced function like facial recognition. But the system found obvious stuff instantly and the search on anti-drone systems found a press release from a small Brazilian security company:

> CDS (Castillo Defence Systems) has sold our proven drone defence equipment to more than twenty prisons around the world, including famous institutions such as San Quentin, Bang Kwang, the São Paulo House of Detention and Pelican Island.

'Result!' Robin told himself.

But as he started a deep dive into how CDS's technology worked, he glanced at the time and almost had a heart attack. 'Josie'll skin me!' Robin blurted, standing up so fast his wheeled office chair clattered into the workstation behind.

He made the four-hundred-metre dash across the casino floor and up twenty-four flights of stairs to the Sherwood Castle penthouse in about two seconds. As he stumbled into the swanky penthouse kitchen, Karma was giving baby Zack a bath in the sink, while Matt Maid scraped leftovers and eight-year-old Otto loaded the dishwasher.

'Josie says you're a loser,' Otto blurted cheerfully. 'And I ate your trifle.'

'Balls!' Robin moaned, then slumped against the fridge holding his ribs as he caught his breath.

As Robin tried to leave, Indio blocked the kitchen doorway. 'Hold on, mister,' she snapped. 'Where were you all afternoon?'

'Explain later,' Robin gasped. 'Got to find Josie.'

'Mr Khan messaged me,' Indio said sternly. 'Apparently, you skipped lessons and didn't hand in your science project.'

'It's not on, Robin,' Karma added, as she gently sponged Zack's head. 'How many times have we talked about the importance of homework and school?'

'I . . .' Robin squirmed, as Otto hid behind Karma and poked out his tongue. 'I'll do all my work this weekend, OK? But Josie's angry *now*. I've got to find her.'

Rather than barge Indio out of the doorway, Robin exited the kitchen by a side door that led into a laundry room. Then he ran along the marble hallway towards the penthouse exit with Indio yelling after him.

'Robin Hood, if you *dare* leave this apartment—'

Robin dared.

He didn't know where Josie was, but once he'd run down enough stairs to be sure Indio wasn't chasing, he pulled his phone. He felt grumpy, knowing he'd have to go back and face Karma and Indio later. Then he felt like a stalker, opening a tracking app and using it to locate Josie's phone.

She'd gone down to Sherwood Castle's Mexican restaurant, Tortilla Durango. The joint hadn't served food since the rebels took over, but it had become a teen hangout.

The posh downstairs dining area had been wrecked by summer floods and kids had added to the post-apocalyptic vibe by catapulting stones through windows and nuking everything from floor tiles to ceiling fans with graffiti.

'All hail the mighty hero,' a fifteen-year-old emo kid called Marvin carped, as Robin ran in and got a lungful of cigarette smoke.

A girl with messy, blue-streaked hair picked a beer bottle off the floor. 'You want a beer, Robin?' she asked. 'Or drugs?'

'Hard drugs,' said another girl, sprawled across two dining tables in laddered black stockings.

'We should get Robin high and post a video,' Marvin said, in a smartass tone that rubbed Robin the wrong way.

The emo trio found themselves hilarious, but Robin knew Marvin and the girls from School Zone and they were about as hardcore as a hamster.

'What did you have, two puffs and half a beer?' Robin teased as he glanced around. 'Have you seen Josie?'

'Try the booths,' the girl sprawled over the tables said. 'Upstairs.'

Marvin made another snarky remark as Robin jogged away. 'Please may I have your autograph, Robin Hood? I've watched all your videos. It's *so* special to meet you.'

'You know there's CCTV in here, Marvin?' Robin said. 'Imagine if someone who knew how to hack computers *accidentally* sent your dad a clip of you smoking.'

Marvin shot up like a bolt. 'That's not cool, man.'

Robin walked backwards and made peace signs as he reached a set of spiral stairs. 'Don't worry, Marv. I'm groovy.'

As Robin hurried up spiral stairs, he looked down at mounds of bottles and junk food packaging. The restaurant's upper level had circular booths with high-backed leather seats. Most were empty, but a few held lively groups of kids, including one big group playing board games.

The lights up here didn't work, so most illumination came from phone screens. Robin's tracking app wasn't accurate enough to pinpoint Josie, and he disturbed two lads kissing when he peeked into a dark booth.

'Buzz off!' one guy shouted, lobbing something heavy in Robin's direction.

It was too dark to easily recognise Josie, and darker still as Robin neared the back wall. Finally, he spotted Alan's distinctive afro sticking over the top of a booth and realised Josie was with him.

In his panic, Robin hadn't considered what to say. Rather than blurt something idiotic, he ducked into an empty booth to think.

Keep it simple. Tell Josie I'm sorry and take whatever she throws at me.

But I made a promise earlier, so she won't buy that . . .

Why didn't I set an alarm when I got to the Nest?

'Hang on,' Josie said. 'Alan, wait. Stop kissing.'

What?

What?

Robin felt like an elephant stood on his chest as he tried to grasp what Josie just said. He'd definitely heard 'Stop kissing', but it wasn't harsh, like Alan was forcing her.

'We can't keep doing this,' Josie told Alan. 'Robin's your best friend.'

Robin tried to breathe, but now he had several elephants on his chest.

'He's never around,' Alan said, as Robin slid deeper into his booth to hear better. 'You said you'd break up with him.'

Robin watched Alan's afro tilt, like he was moving in for another kiss. Then there was a creak as Josie slid across the leather booth away from him. Robin saw her hand come up over the top as she flicked her hair off her face.

'I'll break up with Robin tomorrow,' Josie said.

'You said that days ago,' Alan answered.

'I could hardly upset Robin while he was working to sabotage Marjorie's campaign.'

'Can we forget Robin for five minutes?' Alan groaned. 'I have raging hormones to deal with.'

Josie laughed, which somehow hurt Robin more than the kissing. He wanted to dive over the booth and punch the crap out of his supposed best friend, but the shock was so bad Robin could barely lift one arm.

'Robin will see me tomorrow before school,' Josie said. 'He'll make his usual promises about spending more time with me and less time trying to save the world. But this time I'll break up with him, OK?'

'Cool,' Alan said. 'But don't mention me. Give it a couple of weeks. Then we'll act like we got together after the break-up.'

'More sneaking about,' Josie moaned.

'You've seen the size of the weights Robin throws around in the gym,' Alan replied. 'And it would be a tragedy if he damaged my beautiful face.'

Josie gave her loudest laugh yet. 'Go on, kiss me before I change my mind.'

As Josie and Alan slid down the booth and started making out again, Robin gathered enough strength to stand up and stumble back towards the spiral stairs. Nothing would ever hurt Robin as much as the day his mum died, but this didn't feel far off.

11. BEDTIME FUN

It was 7:40pm. Lockdown began at eight and Stable Block's cockroach-infested washroom was packed with half-dressed inmates taking their last chance to shower, brush their hair and use a sit-down toilet before being locked in their cells for eleven hours.

Freya and a couple of the biggest girls in Marion's cell blocked off the washbasin in one corner while Marion cleaned her teeth. In the opposite corner, the new inmate Marion had seen getting bullied squatted tearfully against the mouldy tiles, the neck of her prison-issue T-shirt ripped open.

Mafia 13 girls had stolen everything the new arrival owned and banished her from her own cell. But when lockdown happened, she'd have to go in the cell and they'd start on her again.

Marion hated that she'd got so used to inmates being bullied that she barely noticed. But she tried to ward off dark thoughts as she flicked water off her toothbrush and stepped aside to let Sophie use the crusty sink.

Marion knew she was lucky to be in a cell where she had friends, and if she got through the next twenty minutes, she'd be safe in her bed for eleven hours. But after what happened in meat processing earlier, it wasn't a question of whether Mafia 13 would kick off, but of when and how bad it would be.

'Sophie, hurry up!' Freya urged.

As a member of the gang Freya had jokingly named the Super Seven came out of a toilet, a girl from another cell tried to go in.

'Don't you dare,' Freya barked.

'I *really* need to go,' the girl begged.

'Not my problem!' Freya said, staring the girl down as Sophie stepped into the doorless cubicle.

As the girl desperately sought a cubicle that wasn't being cordoned off by a gang, a crowd of Mafia 13 girls surged into the washroom. Inmates with no one to look out for them hurried out, even with soapy hands or mouths full of toothpaste.

The helpless new girl moaned as gang members pulled her up by her hair, but Mafia 13 weren't here for the newbie. Marion felt a shiver down her back as the thugs blocked the Super Seven into their corner.

'Reparations,' a tattooed monster nicknamed Ice Lolly told Freya, then pointed at Marion. 'Hand over the freak and we'll leave you alone.'

Freya shook her head as the Super Seven formed a wall, with Marion behind it.

'Marion's my flesh-and-blood cousin,' Freya said, as she looked up the monster's nostrils. 'You come for her, you come for me.'

'For all of us,' Marion's friend Lola added.

'Can you count?' Ice Lolly asked, as her gang-mates snickered. 'We're bigger and there's more of us.'

'Gonna smash you!' a girl up back added, as she clanked something heavy against a sink.

Freya pushed her hand down the front of her shorts and came out with a crude metal bracelet wrapped over her knuckles.

'Less words, more blood!' an impatient girl wedged in the Mafia 13 pack snarled, then gave Ice Lolly a two-handed shove into Freya.

As Freya destroyed Ice Lolly's nose with her knuckleduster, someone charged low at Sophie, grabbing her around the thighs and flipping her over her shoulder. As Freya threw punches and bloodied at least two more noses, the sheer number of Mafia 13 bodies forced her back towards the sinks, leaving Marion exposed.

Marion backed into a toilet stall. There was no door, but there were partitions between cubicles, so she stood on the seatless metal toilet, put her hands on top of the partitions and delivered an almighty two-footed kick at the first girl who got close.

This bought Marion a few seconds. But as Stable Block's emergency alarm erupted, she got yanked out of the cubicle, then dragged across wet floor tiles while Mafia 13 girls kicked punched and tore at her hair.

It could have been worse, but the cramped space and number of attackers meant limbs got tangled and blows didn't connect. Marion glimpsed Freya, still on her feet throwing punches. Sophie had a bloody nose and Lola was sinking her teeth into Ice Lolly's tattooed foot.

'SWAT's coming!' a Mafia 13 lookout shouted from the hallway.

To save money, King Corporation ran cell blocks with just two guards for every hundred inmates. But when things kicked off, a six-person SWAT team was never far away.

SWAT was an acronym for Special Weapons And Tactics. The Pelican Island website said these elite officers were trained to bring dangerous or violent situations under control using minimal force. Unofficially, every inmate knew that if you found yourself in a room with a SWAT team, you were going to get battered.

As the Mafia 13 girls nearest the door scrambled out to take refuge in their cells, the six SWAT officers charged Stable Block's main corridor, dressed in gas masks and black riot protection gear, shouting, 'Get down!' as they drummed their fifty-thousand-volt stun sticks against the inside of clear plastic riot shields.

Lola was the last girl to escape the washroom, snagging her foot between a barred gate and an advancing shield, then breaking free and scrambling down the hallway to the Super Sevens' cell.

The SWAT leader ripped a can of tear gas from her belt and threw it to the back of the bathroom. As the gas burned eyes and made girls choke, the SWAT team with their wall of riot shields pressed battling girls into the rear wall.

Marion saw blood on her hand as Ice Lolly and the new girl both collapsed on top of her.

'Fry, piglets,' one SWAT officer shouted maniacally as he opened a gap between shields and used his extra-long stun stick to zap everything he touched.

The tear gas erupting in the enclosed space made it hard to see and harder to breathe, but somehow Freya stayed on her feet, punching and kicking Ice Lolly, then stepping on a sink, diving onto a riot shield and trapping a SWAT officer beneath it.

As the line of riot shields broke down, the new girl managed to grasp the shaft of a stun stick, tear it away from its owner then jab the dangerous end into Ice Lolly's neck. The stun stick clattered to the ground as the biggest SWAT officer grabbed the new girl and slammed her against a sink.

Ice Lolly now seemed to be unconscious. Her weight was mostly slumped on top of Marion, who didn't mind because it protected her from kicks and blows thrown by SWAT officers.

Sophie got dragged out into the hall with a bloody nose and tears streaking her face. As one officer threw her down and bound her wrists and ankles with plastic cuffs, another yanked Ice Lolly out of the washroom by her ankles.

Marion saw that Freya was still on her feet, despite two huge officers trying to knock her down by kicking the backs of her legs. When Freya finally buckled, a SWAT officer twisted her arms behind to fit cuffs, but the team leader barked an order.

'That one needs to be taught a lesson – break her arm.'

Marion was hurting from getting worked over by Mafia 13, plus choking and half-blind from the tear gas. If she'd kept playing dead, she probably would have got away with a couple of kicks before being cuffed and marched to a punishment cell. But her life in Pelican Island would have been a hundred times harder if her cousin hadn't stuck up for her, and she couldn't stand by while SWAT officers broke Freya's arm.

The plan came together as fast as Marion could think. The stun baton that the new girl snatched was still on the floor. SWAT officers' riot gear protected them from getting shocked, but Freya had twisted one officer's helmet off during their tussle, leaving exposed skin at the back of his neck.

'You're scum!' Marion shouted, as she used the wall as a kickboard to skid across the floor and snatch the stun stick. Then she found her feet and jammed the stick into the officer's neck.

Marion's sense of triumph lasted less than a second. As the guard she'd zapped collapsed to his knees, the team leader grabbed Marion's T-shirt, bounced her off the wall then blasted her face with half a can of pepper spray.

'Think you can try it on with us?' the leader roared down Marion's ear, as Freya got dragged out.

Marion didn't hear, because she'd passed out from the pain.

12. MIDNIGHT HIDEOUT

Robin couldn't face the penthouse and another argument about school, so he went to the Nest. It was the first place adults would come looking, so he set a laptop to access the Super remotely, then went down to the casino floor and hid in a cashier's booth.

This was where casino gamblers used to buy chips for table games, or cash in winning tickets. The carpet was super bouncy and Robin felt cosy as he hid in the footwell behind the counter.

Robin sulked, closing his eyes and imagining he could fall asleep and never have to wake up and face everyone. But every time he thought about Alan and Josie kissing, he felt queasy, like everything was floating around in his stomach. Part of him wanted to cry because the betrayal hurt so bad, while his angry side wanted to smash stuff up.

He felt exhausted, but his thoughts went too fast to sleep. He opened up the laptop to check what the Super had done with the searches from earlier. The machine ran the latest version of the internet retailer TwoTu's data lake software. Its artificial intelligence algorithms were creepily good – not just at searching for words, but at grasping what you were trying to find.

Robin's first search for maps of Pelican Island only found outline maps, where details had been blacked out for security. But while Robin might have given up, the Super made thousands more queries.

One led the Super to a video game company that had made a realistic prison escape game. A disgruntled programmer had posted the game's source code and development archive after getting fired, and this archive included detailed architectural drawings of Pelican Island, down to the locations of water pipes and electrical sockets.

The Super's deep dive into Pelican Island staff also got results. Every major bank gets hacked, so the Super had scoured trillions of bank records in its data lake and found anyone who'd received wages from Pelican Island prison in the last ten years.

With a few clicks, Robin sorted the data and made a list of Pelican Island employees, showing how long they'd worked there, how much they earned and where they lived.

Cut-Throat mentioned that corrupt prison staff were often involved in smuggling, so Robin set the Super to search employees for signs that they had lots of money. It scanned bank records for large savings, vehicle databases for luxury cars and airline passenger data for signs of exotic trips.

It was the kind of puzzle-solving Robin loved, but though it killed time until he could barely stay awake, his brain kept getting swamped by excruciating images of Josie and Alan.

Robin ignored messages from Karma and Indio, but he did answer the yellow emergency radio that he carried everywhere when the duty security officer, Ísbjörg, bleeped him.

'Gisborne put the bounty on your head up to a million,' Ísbjörg reminded him over the radio. 'People get scared when you vanish.'

'Sure,' Robin said and was surprised to find his voice breaking, close to tears.

'What's the matter?' Ísbjörg asked. 'Are you safe?'

'I'm safe,' Robin confirmed, then made a big sniffing sound. 'But my life is a mess.' Robin was embarrassed that he'd sobbed in front of Ísbjörg, a twenty-two-year-old who he barely knew.

'Can't be that bad,' Ísbjörg said soothingly. 'Lots of people care about you. Can you talk it over with Indio or Karma?'

'They still blame me for Marion getting caught.' Robin sniffed again. 'They're always on my back about school and homework, and I stormed off when Indio ordered me not to. My girlfriend's furious 'cos I haven't been spending time with her. Then I found her snogging my best mate.'

'Ouch!' Ísbjörg said, then after a pause to think, 'Robin, I see why you're upset. But it's almost one in the morning. People are worried, and I don't like you being alone when you're feeling sad. How about you go back to the penthouse to sort things out?'

Robin tutted. 'Alan sleeps in my room. If I see that idiot, I'll kick his teeth out.'

'You won't,' Ísbjörg said, annoying Robin with the conviction in her voice.

'You don't know me,' Robin growled, tempted to switch off the radio or tell Ísbjörg to get lost.

'I don't know you *well*,' Ísbjörg explained. 'But you're not a sadist like Guy Gisborne. You wouldn't hurt someone unless they threatened you or someone you cared about.'

'So, on top of everything else I'm a wimp,' Robin moaned, then glanced up as a torch beam shot through the glass in the service counter above his head.

The door at the side of the booth clicked open and Ísbjörg stood in her rebel security camouflage jacket, torch in one hand, walkie-talkie in the other. She switched her radio to another frequency as Robin squinted in the torchlight.

'Tell Indio I've found Robin, and he's fine.'

'I'm not a baby,' Robin told Ísbjörg irritably. 'You didn't have to come looking.'

Ísbjörg smiled. 'You'd also say you were fine if some bad guy held a gun to your head. So here I am, doing my job.'

Robin wondered how she'd found him as he stood up. 'My phone's untraceable. Did you use my radio to track me?'

'Nothing so sophisticated.' Ísbjörg laughed as she pointed to the back of the booth. 'The casino's dark and the light from your laptop screen reflected off the wall.'

'Smart,' Robin admitted as he wiped tears on his sleeve. 'Sorry I've wasted your time.'

'Actually, you saved me from twelve brain-numbing hours at the front desk. Do you feel any better?'

Robin managed a half-smile. 'Still terrible.'

'Getting cheated on is the worst,' Ísbjörg said soothingly. 'First time?'

Robin nodded. 'First proper girlfriend.'

'There's vegan hot chocolate in the security office,' Ísbjörg said. 'If you like, I can make two mugs and tell you stories about all the boys who've broken my heart.'

'Thanks,' Robin said, not sure if Ísbjörg was joking. 'But I guess Karma and Indio have sat up worrying about me.'

'They care about you,' Ísbjörg reminded him. 'A lot.'

'Can't hide forever,' Robin said, as he gave a deep sigh. 'I'll go back to the penthouse and try not to murder Alan.'

13. INDETERMINATE SENTENCE

Marion awoke in a single cell filled with blazing white light. She had a dozen bruises, one shoe, ripped shorts, stinging eyes and a big cut on her hand that was scabbing over.

Her knee buckled when she got up from the bed to get water from the metal sink. There was no cup, so she knelt on the concrete floor, letting drips from the tap hit her tongue, while trying to ignore the vile-smelling toilet alongside.

The windowless punishment cell gave no sense of time. There were shouts and bangs from nearby cells, but mostly men and nobody she recognised. When the cell's solid door clanked and opened, Danielle, the thuggish guard who ran Stable Block, came in wearing clean uniform and fresh make-up. Marion guessed she was starting a morning shift.

'A gift,' Danielle said, as she dropped a little spray bottle filled with milk into Marion's lap. 'The alkali neutralises pepper spray.'

Marion sprayed the milk in her eyes and mouth. It was like being able to scratch the worst itch she'd ever had. 'That's good,' she said, tipping back her head as the milk streaked down her face.

'May I sit?' Danielle asked.

Mean guards like Danielle never asked for a prisoner's permission. Milk and politeness meant she was after something.

Marion felt weak and grotty as the guard sat on the shiny plastic mattress, close enough to knock her sideways.

'Remind me of your sentence,' Danielle said.

'Indeterminate,' Marion said, as she sprayed more milk in her right eye.

'Do you know what that means?' Danielle asked.

Marion nodded. 'I'm a kid, so the judge said she couldn't give me a fixed sentence because I'll grow up and change. They'll review my behaviour every couple of years and decide when I can get out.'

Danielle nodded. 'And who do they ask about your character?'

Marion gave the answer Danielle was fishing for. 'You?'

'Clever girl,' Danielle said. 'If you ever want to get off Pelican Island, you need me on your side. And let's face it, you need every friend you can get right now.'

Marion nodded reluctantly.

'It's an achievement.' Danielle smiled. 'In one day, you burned two members of a ruthless gang. Then you took down a SWAT team member with a stun stick, so every guard will be on your back too.'

Marion knew, but hearing it from Danielle still made her shudder.

'I'll make your life easier if you help me clean up the mess.'

'How?' Marion asked reluctantly.

'When something kicks off, like last night in the washroom, I wind up with a whole stack of paperwork. I'll have to spend my next three shifts writing incident reports, organising repairs, searching cells for weapons, and dealing with senior staff who want to know why a mini-riot broke out in my washroom.

'Trouble is, we have one gang too many in Stable Block. There won't be order until I break up the Super Seven. If you sign a statement saying that Freya and Sophie have been selling drugs—'

'Are you insane?' Marion interrupted furiously, as she slid herself down the bed, away from Danielle. 'First, I'm no snitch. Second, it's not Super Seven that causes trouble. That girl who arrived yesterday got battered by Mafia 13 and robbed of everything except the clothes on her back. You've got CCTV, so why didn't you stop that?'

'Don't forget who you are talking to, inmate,' Danielle snapped, then gripped the back of Marion's shirt and shoved her off the bed with enough force to make her hit the opposite wall and stumble. 'This isn't a holiday camp. There will always be bullying and gangs.'

Marion groaned and rolled onto her back as Danielle planted her steel-capped boot in front of her face.

'You've got too many enemies,' Danielle warned. 'I could move you to a cell with eight girls from Mafia 13 who will make your life hell. Or you can save yourself. Give me two scapegoats to show my bosses, nip gang war in Stable Block in the bud. In return, I'll make sure nobody touches you – and fix you up with an easy job. Prison shop, library, whatever you fancy.'

Marion glowered defiantly up at the guard. 'I'd rather get stabbed than snitch on my friends.'

'Let's see how you feel after a couple of days in here.' Danielle laughed, as she made Marion flinch with a tiny shift of her boot. 'You'll be begging me for help.'

14. STUPID BREAK-UP SONGS

It was 2am when Robin stumbled meekly into the penthouse. Karma and Indio had waited up. They said they were sorry about what had happened with Josie, but would still have to talk about school stuff in the morning.

Robin couldn't face seeing Alan, so he found a tatty throw and crashed on the living-room couch in the clothes he'd been wearing all day. He got woken at six by Finn Maid, who snuggled up to him, watching cartoons on the giant projector while Robin wished his life was as simple as the three-year-old's.

When Indio got up, she diplomatically went and told Alan that Robin had seen him kissing Josie the night before. The entire Maid family knew by breakfast, and it was tense around the table as Robin and Alan sat at opposite ends eating scrambled egg.

Alan messaged Josie telling her that Robin had seen, which made for more awkwardness in the hallway before

School Zone. Alan, Robin and Josie were usually part of a lively group who stood around talking trash. But Robin stood as far from Alan and Josie as he could and their mates had to pick sides before they knew what had happened.

School always went ten times slower than everything else and today was worse. Robin felt less shocked than the night before, but the feeling of being dumped and betrayed was crushing, and the only thing worse than everyone gossiping behind his back was well-meaning kids who said stuff like 'Sorry about the break-up' and 'You'll get over it.'

Robin felt some relief when the most awkward school day of his life ended. He went to the Nest to see how the Super was getting on with Pelican Island research. The supercomputer had now dug up so much stuff that the problem wasn't finding information, but sifting through all the data and working out what was useful for solving Cut-Throat's drone problem.

Robin decided his priority was learning about Pelican Island's anti-drone system. According to Castillo Defence Systems' website, its equipment was cheap, effective and easy to install. It worked by detecting the distinctive sound of an approaching drone, then generating a powerful radio-jamming signal. This blocked communication between the drone and its pilot, along with the GPS signals that drones use to navigate.

Robin felt like he was on familiar ground, because he'd built a device to jam radio signals and make police surveillance drones crash the previous summer. Now he had to find a way to do the opposite.

'Hey, you,' Josie said warily, making Robin jump.

Robin felt like he'd been slugged in the gut as he saw his former girlfriend at the top of the stairs. She wore her School Zone gym shirt and the trashed Adidas trainers that she'd worn forever.

'Had softball after school,' she said. 'Can we talk?'

'Why not?' Robin sighed.

As Josie got close, Robin liked her warm smell and felt an ache when he wanted to kiss her, but couldn't.

'I'm sorry about the way it went down,' Josie began, as she dumped her school bag and sat in one of the office chairs. 'I didn't want to hurt you. But me and Alan were spending all our time together while you were busy. And it turns out, if you take someone who's cute and funny, then mix in rampant teenage hormones, you end up lying on the big penthouse bed making out.'

'On *my* bed?' Robin spluttered.

Josie saw mentioning the bed was a mistake and became a little more aggressive. 'It's not like you were the perfect boyfriend, Robin. And look online. They sell Robin Hood posters on TwoTu. There are *thousands* of girls posting messages about how amazing Robin Hood is. You could have ten girlfriends if you wanted.'

Robin tutted. 'Until they meet me and realise I'm almost fourteen, but shorter than most eleven-year-olds.'

Josie smirked and shook her head. 'Girls are supposed to be the vain ones. But you're *obsessed* with your height, Alan can't leave his hair alone, and he'll only wear those super-long basketball shorts because he thinks his legs are too skinny.'

'True,' Robin admitted. 'I guess we all look in the mirror and fixate on what we don't like.'

'I'm sorry I went behind your back and made a mess of everything,' Josie said, as she rocked her office chair awkwardly. 'I hope we can be friends.'

'I wasn't the best boyfriend,' Robin admitted. 'You can't make promises and not keep them.'

'Friends?' Josie asked pleadingly.

'I need time,' Robin said sadly. 'I've known Alan since nursery, but when I think about him kissing you, I want to smack him in the mouth.'

'Try not to,' Josie urged. 'There's actually something I came here to show you, if you've got time.'

'Kinda busy with drone stuff,' Robin said.

Josie held up two fingers. 'Two minutes,' she promised. She cracked a mischievous smile as she logged into the computer in front of her chair and began an explanation. 'We've been paying our people in Vietnam to do homework for you, me and a few select friends.'

'A few?' Robin laughed. 'You've been selling homework to half of School Zone. It's a miracle you haven't been caught.'

'Trouble is, we get answers but still have to spend ages copying them out in our own handwriting. So,

I wondered if we could make computer fonts that look like handwriting.'

Robin shook his head. 'If I write a word fifty times, it never looks the same twice. Fonts only have one version of each letter.'

'Obviously,' Josie said. 'But I used the Super to look into it. It found a university project where researchers tried to make computers do realistic handwriting. You write each letter of the alphabet ten times in lower-case and capitals. Then you scan it in and the program analyses the result.

'Once everything's set up, you copy and paste text into the program and it makes it look like your real handwriting by making it wonky and changing the letters and stuff. You can even add spelling mistakes.'

'But does it work?' Robin asked.

Josie had already unzipped her backpack, and now pulled out a history essay that had been marked A minus. 'Ta-da!'

Robin grabbed the essay and studied the fake handwriting. 'Looks exactly like yours,' he said.

'If you fill out sample pages, I'll scan them in and set the program up to do your handwriting too,' Josie said.

'Anything to win the war on homework,' Robin said keenly.

'I'll print out the grids for your handwriting sample,' Josie said. 'You can use it for your science project, though you'll still have to draw the pie charts.'

Robin felt OK talking to Josie after blanking her all day at school, but as she reached under the desk to switch on an all-in-one printer, he looked at her hair and her back and breathed through his nose to catch her smell. He wanted his girlfriend back more than he'd ever wanted anything.

'What idiot hid the power switch around the back?' Josie complained.

As Josie crawled under the desk, Robin felt a lump in his throat.

She's beautiful and funny and clever and she dumped me because I went off to mess around with a stupid computer.

I'm the stupidest person in the world for not spending more time with her.

And if I don't get out of here right now, Josie's gonna see me crying my eyes out.

'Are you OK?' Josie asked as Robin scrambled towards the toilet at the back of the Nest.

'Dodgy tummy,' Robin lied, then locked the toilet door and stared at his teary eyes in the mirror over the little sink.

He hadn't realised how badly getting dumped would hurt. As he sat on the toilet, he finally understood why there are so many terrible songs about people cheating or breaking up.

15. THE DEVIL'S FIST

Marion was fuelled by anger while Danielle was in the cell, but once the guard left, she was on her own with nothing but pain. She sat on the bed with her head between her knees, shielding her eyes from blazing light. It was so powerful she could see the blueish veins in her legs as she got sucked into dark thoughts.

Mafia 13 batters and stabs its enemies.

Guards won't protect me after I attacked one of them.

I'm one of the smallest inmates and my leg isn't perfect after the operation.

What if Danielle goes after my friends?

She only needs to get one of us to sign a statement saying that we deal drugs.

Freya's tough, but Sophie's got rich parents and an expensive lawyer.

Lola had a baby when she was fourteen and is desperate to get out and get her kid back.

Will they break if Danielle threatens them with charges that could add years to their sentences?

I hate Danielle's guts, but how can I survive if I don't take the deal?

But then I'd be stitching up Freya, who's looked after me since I got here.

I'd be stitching up my cousin!

'GRRRRRRRR!' Marion moaned as she bunched fists and pounded the mattress.

A creep purred from the next cell. 'Sound sweet when you're angry, little girl.'

Marion was tempted to yell back, but suspected he'd enjoy the attention. Then she heard another inmate walking down the corridor.

'You wouldn't mess with her if you knew who her father is,' the inmate warned.

Marion glanced around as the serving flap in her door clanked open. A meal tray hit the little shelf inside the flap, then a man with a biker's beard put his face through the hole and sounded friendly.

'Lunch,' the guy said. 'How you holding up?'

'Been better,' Marion said, her body aching as she took the tray.

When she saw the food, she recognised special treatment: ham instead of squashy meat paste, a whole baguette, two oranges and single-serve packs of Marmite, jam and honey.

'Don't know your tastes so there's a selection,' the beard said, then raised the cuff of his T-shirt to show a faded tattoo. 'Name's Ted, but most call me Nemo.'

The tat was the logo of Devil's Fist Motorcycle Club. Ironically, Devil's Fist was a sworn enemy of the Brigands Motorcycle Club that Marion's dad belonged to, but inside prison the bike gangs stuck together.

'Cheers,' Marion said, enjoying the feeling that someone cared about her.

'Lucky you ended up here,' Nemo said quietly, as he gestured for Marion to get closer.

'Doesn't feel lucky.' Marion sighed.

'Huge gang fight in the women's exercise yard yesterday afternoon,' Nemo explained. 'When you juveniles kicked off in Stable Block, there wasn't a single female punishment cell available. This is the men's punishment block, where us bikers have influence.'

'This bread is warm,' Marion said.

Nemo nodded. 'Food from the guards' kitchen to get your strength up!'

When Marion picked up the baguette, she uncovered a frosty sandwich bag filled with dense red liquid.

'Is that blood?' Marion gulped, almost dropping the tray.

Nemo nodded, then took a wary glance down the corridor. 'Guard's gonna yell at me to move on, so listen. They're not supposed to keep women in male accommodation, so they'll move you back to Stable Block soon. Eat your lunch, then open that bag of blood and squeeze it over yourself.'

Marion felt squeamish. 'Where?'

'Maybe your arm, because you've already got cuts there. The important thing is to make a mess.'

'Whose blood is it?'

'It's from the hospital blood bank,' Nemo said, as he glanced back again. 'It's filtered and cleaned, so don't worry. When I come back in twenty minutes to collect the trays, I'll see you all bloody and acting like you passed out. I'll call the guard. You act like you're dying and they'll take you to hospital.'

'They'll know I'm faking when they wipe me off.'

Nemo nodded. 'King Corporation's too cheap to pay nurses. It's bikers with first-aid certificates who triage new arrivals at the hospital. We can't keep you there forever, but it'll buy time for guards to calm down and for us to figure out other ways to help you.'

As Nemo predicted, a guard shouted furiously down the hallway. 'Inmate, quit bothering her and serve the lunches.'

'Aye aye, boss,' Nemo shouted, giving the guard a cheeky salute as he backed away, then a quick smile for Marion before slamming the serving hatch.

16. SAUSAGE AND MASH

An hour after Josie left, Robin was still in the Nest. He was reading through research when Indio came up the stairs, holding a tray with sausage and mash, cherry pie, Rage Cola and a side of whipped cream.

'Fab!' Robin said hungrily, but Indio saw his sad eyes as Robin looked away from the screen. 'It's a long walk. You didn't have to.'

Indio surprised Robin by kneeling behind his chair and giving him a hug. 'I know you feel horrible,' she said. 'Learning to deal with break-ups is one of the less fun parts of growing up.'

'I'll be a better boyfriend next time, for sure.'

'I spoke to Alan, and we agreed it's best he moves out of your room.'

Robin looked keen. 'A room ten floors away would suit me.'

Indio shook her head. 'I don't ditch kids I take in, even

when they cause trouble, storm off and set a horrible example to the younger ones.'

Robin smiled guiltily. 'So where is Alan going?'

'He's moving in with Finn. Matt's going to share your room.'

'No way!' Robin huffed, coughing and spitting out food. 'Matt's *insanely* annoying. He's always trying to copy me. And his stupid mates will be in my room acting like idiots and touching my stuff.'

'The penthouse only has three bedrooms. Either share with Matt or sleep on the balcony.'

'I just might.' Robin sighed.

'You're here in the Nest more than you're in your room anyway,' Indio said. 'Now I have to get back to the little ones before rioting breaks out. And it's not healthy sitting here alone for hours. Finish whatever you're doing, then come home. We'll watch TV, or play a game.'

'I'm trying to solve Cut-Throat's drone problem,' Robin said.

Karma thought for a second. 'You have until seven,' she said. 'And you're wearing the clothes you slept in, so take a shower.'

Robin would have preferred to stay in the Nest working on the drone stuff. But he appreciated Indio bringing him food and caring about stuff like showers.

It was twenty to seven and Robin was shutting down his computer when Cut-Throat came up the steps to the Nest.

'Hear your ass got dumped,' Cut-Throat said, with brick-like subtlety.

'How'd you hear that?' Robin asked as Cut-Throat sat in the office chair Josie always used.

The giant dirt-crusted biker laughed. 'People gossip. But don't beat yourself up. A woman is like a beautiful motorbike: great for a while, but they always break down.'

Robin laughed and shook his head. It seemed wild that this oafish biker who compared women to motorbikes had once been married to Karma.

'What's happening about the drones?' Cut-Throat asked, then lifted his leg and ripped an enormous fart.

'Two main threads,' Robin said, trying not to laugh or gag as the Nest was engulfed in a putrid aroma. 'The Super dug up financial information on the prison guards and other staff. I've found at least four prison staff who have *way* more money than they should have.

'The most senior is a deputy warden called Anne Kemp. She lives alone in a nice house on the edge of Sherwood. Two years ago, she was diagnosed with a heart problem. Instead of getting treated here, she flew to a clinic in Switzerland for treatment that cost over two hundred thousand. She keeps a low profile by driving to work in an old SUV, but when she went on holiday last Christmas, she flew first class and spent thousands on room service.'

Cut-Throat roared with laughter. 'I'd love to hear her try to explain that. And if you can get this information in half a day, what's wrong with the police?'

Robin pointed towards the bright green supercomputer in the middle of the room. 'Privacy rules mean cops need to go to court to look at a single bank statement. The Super can access hundreds of stolen bank databases and scan a billion bank statements in minutes.'

'Scary,' Cut-Throat said, eying the machine suspiciously.

Robin nodded. 'Hackers have all the power.'

'What about drones?'

Robin smiled proudly. 'I've found the system installed on Pelican Island and I have a good idea how it works. I also found a government report from a prison in Mexico. I don't speak Spanish and the online translation isn't perfect, but it seems like smugglers in Mexico had no problem beating the system. It detects drones with sound, so if you block the microphones it won't work.'

Cut-Throat pointed at the Super. 'Do you need to be here to use that?'

Robin shook his head. 'I can log in remotely.'

'What's tomorrow?' Cut-Throat asked.

'Friday,' Robin answered.

'I'm meeting a guy here first thing,' Cut-Throat said. 'Got a container-load of high-end watches I need to sell. I'll be leaving for Brigands camp around eleven. There's a fortieth birthday bash at our camp on Friday night. You can take a boat west to Lake Victoria on Saturday, then meet Ollie, get eyes on Pelican Island and try to figure this drone situation.'

'Oh,' Robin said, startled.

'Problem?' Cut-Throat asked.

'You asked me to look into this. I didn't realise you wanted me to go to Lake Victoria.'

'What else are you gonna do all weekend?' Cut-Throat asked. 'Mope about while your best mate is across the hall getting frisky with your ex?'

The remark was close to the bone and even the thuggish Cut-Throat saw the hurt in Robin's eyes.

'Sorry, kid,' Cut-Throat said. 'I was on leave the day Brigands did sensitivity training.'

Robin covered with a laugh before Cut-Throat continued.

'I reckon it'll be good for you. Fresh air, taking on a challenge. And it's all so I can smuggle gear in for Marion.'

'It would be good to get away,' Robin admitted. 'But Karma and Indio are on my back about school I've missed.'

'School,' Cut-Throat scoffed, as he burst out laughing. 'Is Mr Khan on your back again? I'll have one of my guys run him over if you like.'

Robin laughed, though you could never be sure Cut-Throat was joking.

'I was married to Karma for eight years so I know what she's like,' Cut-Throat said. 'If you went to every lesson and got A* on every homework for a year, she'd still find something to complain about.'

'I guess,' Robin said, reluctant to say anything negative about Karma when she'd done so much for him. 'I definitely want to help Marion.'

'You're a free spirit, like me,' Cut-Throat said airily as he stood up and stretched. 'Pack your bag and meet me at the back of the castle at eleven tomorrow morning. Leave Karma and Indio a note, saying you're with me and you're safe. And make sure you bring that set of Brigands colours I gave you. We'll make a biker out of Robin Hood yet!'

17. DO NO HARM

Marion had nothing sharp so had to tear the blood bag open with her teeth. It had been stolen from a freezer and only partly defrosted, so the blood was cold as she let it streak over her wrist, pool on her plastic mattress and drip to the concrete floor.

The scam worked perfectly. Marion played dead, Nemo called the duty guard, and two bikers in faded blue hospital scrubs arrived suspiciously fast.

'Lucky we were nearby,' one biker said. 'Lots of blood for a youngster. Better get her out of here.'

Before the guard could check Marion's pulse or wonder how so much blood had appeared from a small graze, one biker had lifted her onto a trolley, and the other hid the evidence by pocketing the sandwich bag and winding bandage around the fake bleed.

The prison hospital was a five-floor elevator ride and a kilometre walk from the punishment block. It was a juddering trolley ride over rough floors and every few hundred metres they had to stop at barred gates, one behind the other.

These gates needed a guard on both sides, or an intercom call to the prison control room to get the outer gate open. This double-lock system meant inmates couldn't move through the prison, even if they stole keys.

Marion was glad she wasn't really injured, because guards took ages to leave their posts and saunter across to open outer gates. Her leg surgery had been done at a children's hospital outside of prison, so this was her first experience of Pelican Island's medical facilities.

First stop was a triage area, jammed with inmates on trolleys who'd been beaten, stabbed, taken drug overdoses or attempted suicide. Those with minor complaints sat in chairs along the side wall, while overhead was a balcony where an armed guard messed with her phone.

Patients were dealt with by inmates in scrubs with rips and stains. Most were bikers and Marion was fascinated, watching giant tattooed men with nets over long hair and beards. Their manner was brusque, cursing patients who demanded attention or pain relief and even spraying disinfectant in the mouth of a patient who tried to steal scissors from a supply cabinet.

But while sympathy ran short, the bikers seemed remarkably competent. Stitching, bandaging, handing out pills. There was a duty paramedic giving advice on more complex cases, and a frazzled-looking surgical team that rushed out when a guy arrived suffering a heart attack.

After a couple of hours amidst the madness, a biker wheeled Marion past several wards of male patients.

'See this scar?' the biker said, smiling as he raised the sleeve of his scrubs. 'Your old man did that with a broken bottle.'

'What a small world,' Marion said awkwardly as she looked up, watching ceiling tiles whizz by.

'Few years later my bike got stolen. Cut-Throat held no grudge. He put out word in the motor trade. Got my bike back with minor damage and the name of the guy who stole it.'

Marion smiled as she looked around and realised they'd reached a female ward. 'My dad says there's a special place in hell for bike thieves.'

'Thief was in hell when we got hold of him,' the biker said, laughing fondly at the memory. 'Your dad's an important guy, so if his little girl wants something, she just gotta ask.'

'Appreciate that,' Marion said, as the biker rolled her trolley up beside an empty bed.

'Want me to lift you?' the biker asked.

Marion shook her head, but made sure nobody was looking before hopping easily onto the bed. She had two big pillows and a proper mattress that was paradise compared to the crumbling foam she slept on in Stable Block.

'See you around, Marion,' the biker said, then looked across at an inmate in faded pink scrubs. 'Lydia, is there tea and cake for my friend here?'

Marion adjusted her pillows, enjoyed the smell of fresh bed linen, and looked at the elderly woman in the next bed. She was unconscious and the drip bag hanging over her bed had a big yellow sticker that said **FOLFOX CHEMOTHERAPY – DISPOSE OF SAFELY**.

After an instant of pity for an old lady with cancer, Marion smiled as Lydia rested a tray with a generous slice of Victoria sponge and a metal mug of tea on Marion's bedside table.

'Sugar?'

'Two,' Marion said.

Lydia smiled as she plopped sugar cubes in Marion's mug. She fished out the teabag, then kept smiling as she grabbed Marion's unbandaged left arm and pressed the teaspoon that had been standing in the hot tea against the back of her hand.

Lydia tightened her grip as Marion yelped and tried to pull away. The spoon was only hot enough to leave a red mark, but when Lydia let go, she flashed Marion the back of her wrist, which had the number thirteen tattooed on it.

'I saw those girls you hit with the steam wand before they took them to outside hospital,' Lydia said nastily. 'Too many bikers in here, but your fake wound won't keep you safe for long.'

18. ONE O'CLOCK SHARP

There were some advantages to sharing a room with Matt Maid. First, the eleven-year-old's nose didn't make the annoying whistling sound that Alan's did when he was asleep. Second, Robin's bathroom was no longer cluttered with Alan's collection of zit creams, fancy soaps and hair mousse.

But the honeymoon ended an hour before school on Friday morning. Robin came back from the laundry room with an armful of clean clothes and Matt got in his way.

'Where are you sneaking off to?' Matt asked.

'Who says I'm sneaking off?'

Matt moved sideways to block him as Robin tried to get to his bed.

'You were up early cleaning archery gear and you put toothbrush and deodorant in your pack.'

Robin tutted. 'I'm surprised you know what deodorant is.'

'Funny,' Matt said dryly. 'Tell me where you're going.'

'None of your business.'

'A-ha!' Matt said. 'So, you are going somewhere.'

'Being annoying isn't compulsory.'

Matt stopped Robin getting by again. This time, Robin dropped his armful of clothes, then got up in the younger boy's face.

'I'm not scared of you!' Matt said confidently.

Matt was three years younger, but even after Robin's recent growth spurt, they were the same height. But Matt was skinny and his confidence drained as he noticed the size of Robin's bicep.

Matt flinched and fled as Robin threw a fake punch. 'I'll tell my mums!' he blurted.

Robin didn't want to hurt Matt, but his bratty new room-mate had to know who was boss. He shoved Matt to the wall, then grasped the elastic around his pyjama bottoms and flung him onto the bed.

Matt suddenly realised that Robin was strong enough to hurt him, but Robin squashed Matt's head down into the bed to stop him yelling and instead of thumping him he dug two fingers under Matt's ribs and tickled.

'Stop!' Matt squealed.

'Are you going to keep your mouth shut?'

'Let me go,' Matt said, but Robin tickled for five more seconds to make a slobbering mess out of him. 'OK, please! Stop! Robin, I won't snitch. I'm just messing.'

Now Matt was at his mercy, Robin decided to have fun.

'Truth is, I'm sneaking off to a house party with some kids I know in Locksley,' Robin lied as he let Matt up. 'Now we're room-mates, I guess you could hang with us.'

Matt wiped a trickle of drool on his sleeve and grinned as he rolled off the bed. 'Really?'

'Sure,' Robin agreed. 'Pack an overnight bag. I've got stuff to do in the Nest, but I'll meet you at the back of the building at one o'clock.'

Now Matt looked wary. 'Indio and Karma will go nuts.'

'It's gonna be a wild party with cool people,' Robin said casually. 'But you're young, so no biggie if you're chicken.'

'I'm not chicken,' Matt said, as Robin got on with packing his bag. 'They'll only ground me, and that's nothing.'

'One o'clock, sharp,' Robin reminded Matt, as he headed out to get breakfast.

Robin waited in his room until the younger kids had left for school. He wrote the first line of a note for Karma and Indio like Cut-Throat suggested, but Robin felt bad and found Karma on the sofa reading a book about tropical fish.

'I'm meeting Cut-Throat at eleven,' Robin told her. 'Going to Pelican Island to try and help solve his drone problem. If we can reopen the smuggling route, we can get stuff to Marion. Hopefully a phone so we can talk to her.'

Karma lowered her book and seemed peeved. 'Sounds like you're telling me, not asking permission.'

'I have to get out of here,' Robin explained. 'After Josie and stuff . . .'

Karma smiled wisely. 'Robin, the thing about running away from your problems is that they're always waiting for you when you get back.'

'I'm not running away,' Robin protested.

'I can't wrestle you to the ground to stop you,' Karma said. 'But remember who you're teaming up with.'

'What's that supposed to mean?' Robin asked. 'Cut-Throat's Marion's dad. He cares about her as much as we do.'

'No doubt,' Karma agreed. 'Cut-Throat can turn on the charm when he needs something, but never forget he's the ruthless leader of a motorbike gang. I'm just warning you to watch your step.'

'Fair,' Robin said, as he shrugged off the warning. 'I'll be back in a few days and I'll let you know how it's going.'

19. BARBECUE AND SEWAGE

A forty-minute hike brought Robin, Cut-Throat and three armed bodyguards to Brigands Motorcycle Club's Sherwood Forest base.

While Emma and Will Scarlock ran the rebel operation at Sherwood Castle with rotas, security protocols and facilities such as the medical centre and School Zone, the Brigands preferred anarchy.

The bikers' previous base had been destroyed by a mudslide the summer before, along with precious bikes and possessions. They'd sensibly picked high ground for their new one. It centred on the overgrown parking lot of a boarding house that once provided some of the forest's most spectacular views.

While most Forest People built shelters from found materials, or lived in abandoned buildings, the Brigands stole a bulldozer and used it to open up twelve hundred metres of single-track road between their hilltop camp and Old Road.

One drunk Brigand then drove the bulldozer into one of its own holes, and the machine was now a trash-filled monument in front of the crumbling boarding house. Around this centrepiece, seventy Brigands lived with their families in a maze of trucks, camper vans and metal shipping containers.

'Look who's here,' Cut-Throat roared as he approached a flaming barbecue pit.

Robin ducked under laundry strung from the power lines that fanned like spider webs from generators at the rear of the site. The air had an enticing aroma of charcoal-grilled meat, but gusts brought a stomach-churning smell from toilets that had been dug too close to the edge of camp.

Cut-Throat had insisted that Robin wore the oversized, filthy denim jacket he'd gifted him the first time they met. The rear had the Brigands MC logo, which meant Robin was a member of the gang.

As Robin surveyed the camp, his jacket ticked loads of people off. From new Brigands members who had to spend two years doing chores and getting picked on before gaining full membership, to boys who couldn't join until they were seventeen, and girls who couldn't join at all.

But Robin was safe while Cut-Throat was close, and plenty of Brigands slapped Robin on the back and asked to have selfies with the young hero. Just after 1pm, Robin was tucking into baked potato and a slab of beef ribs when he got a snarky text message from Matt:

> Think UR clever?
> I'll get you back.

As the afternoon wore on, Robin chased and kicked a ball with Cut-Throat's toddler daughter, Gemma. She was a sweet, if grubby, kid and her wild laugh and thirst for attention helped Robin to take his mind off homework and getting dumped.

When a stolen supermarket truck arrived, Robin helped Brigands and their partners unpack booze, eggs and meat. But he almost swallowed his tongue when a dreadlocked woman in bike leathers handed him a giant birthday cake with an inscription that read:

> Happy Birthday Rob — Here's to 40 more
> years of INSANITY. Insane Rob!

The Brigands and Sherwood Castle rebels were mostly on friendly terms. But individual Brigands made money any way they could, and some worked for bad people.

When Robin last encountered Insane Rob, the biker had been a bodyguard for a group linked to the Russian mafia and Robin's pals had stripped his warm clothes and left him facing a barefoot hike in thick snow.

As Robin decided to keep his distance from the birthday boy, it became clear that the bash was going to be huge. Wooden pallets were stacked up to make a giant hilltop bonfire. When guests began arriving, a few came on boats from a tributary of the Macondo River that ran near the bottom of the hill, but most were sweary back-slapping Brigands on snarling motorbikes.

Brigands all wore the same logo as the one on Robin's back, but the chapter names written under the logo were different: Liverpool, Nottingham, Capital City, Glasgow, and even exotic Brigands from New York, Berlin and Auckland.

Cut-Throat offered Robin beer to drown his sorrows, but Robin didn't like the taste and stuck to Coke. After a couple of cans and another stack of barbecued meat, Robin needed to pee and headed into trees near the edge of camp.

It was nearly dark and the bonfire was kicking into life as he walked back. When he passed between two rows of metal container homes, a line of five kids stepped in front of him.

Brigand kids tended to be big, like their biker fathers. They rarely washed, had never sat in a dentist's chair, didn't go to school and most were tough fighters and superb motorbike riders.

'Nice jacket,' a girl who pushed herself to the front said. 'Pity you didn't earn it.'

She looked about fourteen, though it was hard to tell with the dirt and fading light. Her hair was cropped and she had a massive hunting knife on her belt.

Robin glanced over his shoulder and saw three more kids boxing him in.

'Mr Robin Hood!' a kid of thirteen said, as he came up behind. 'Mr Hero. Mr Save the World. Mr Doesn't Have to Work for Brigand Colours.'

'Cut-Throat gave me this jacket before I knew what it was,' Robin said nervously. 'Would any of you snub Cut-Throat if he gave you something?'

'You're the reason my cousin Marion is locked up,' the girl said, as she stepped closer. 'I'm not impressed with you, Hood.'

The other kids murmured in agreement.

'Take those colours off so I can fight you,' the boy added.

Robin remembered the bikers' code: if you attacked someone wearing gang colours you attacked the whole gang. These kids wouldn't lay a hand on him while he wore the jacket.

One girl had pulled out a phone to film.

'I don't want trouble,' Robin said, stepping forward and hoping the line of bodies would part.

But the girl bumped him and tutted. 'He's small and weak,' she spat, as she looked at the kid filming. 'He's not going to defend himself. Like he didn't defend Marion Maid.'

'Marion was biker tough, not like you,' another kid said.

'He's so short, no wonder his girlfriend dumped him.'

This made everyone except Robin laugh. He was sensitive about his height and furious that the entire world knew he'd been dumped.

'I'll fight,' Robin spat furiously, pulling off the jacket and hardly believing the words exiting his own mouth. 'I'll fight you all at once if I have to.'

This would have been suicidal, so Robin was relieved when everyone except the gobby boy backed away, leaving a circle to fight in.

'This'll get untold views,' the girl filming laughed.

Robin's thoughts raced and it was like his brain had split in three. One part was an adrenaline-fuelled warrior who wanted to work out frustration with his fists. One was the undersized kid who pitied himself and felt like he deserved a beating because he'd let Marion get caught. Last came the voice of sanity, looking down from above, screaming, 'Stop being dumb and run away!'

But the anger dominated. The instant Robin let go of the jacket, his opponent charged. A full head taller than Robin, he threw a blizzard of jabs that suggested he'd done regular boxing. One punch hit Robin painfully in the ribs, but Robin dodged fast. The next punch glanced harmlessly through Robin's tangled hair and made the kid overbalance.

Robin sent his opponent sprawling by sweeping out his legs and following up with a combo that sent him crashing into the dirt. Robin loomed over his opponent, making it clear he'd thump him again if he tried to get up. As the kid groaned and tasted blood from a split lip, Robin worried that the other Brigand kids would pile in.

Everyone but Marion's cousin stayed back.

'Decent for a little guy,' she told Robin, as she reached out to shake hands. 'Might be snoggable if you were older.'

Robin was easily flattered. As he took the girl's hand, he looked her over and saw beauty beneath the dirt.

'What's your name?' Robin asked.

Instead of shaking, the girl gripped Robin's wrist and expertly twisted his arm up behind his back.

As Robin groaned in pain, she drove him forward, slamming him noisily into the corrugated metal side of a container, landed several hard punches and finally flung him to the ground.

For a finishing flourish, she planted her boot on Robin's cheek and wiped dirt on his face.

'That was for what you did to cousin Marion,' she said fiercely. 'And my name is *The Girl Who Just Kicked Your Ass.*'

20. TRENDING NOW

One laughing teen dumped Robin's Brigand colours on top of him as he lay in the dirt catching his breath.

'Put 'em back on before another girl batters you,' he advised.

Robin propped himself against the side of the shipping container as the Brigand kids vanished into the dark. He hurt everywhere and by the time he'd wiped whatever was on the girl's boot off his face and made sure his phone wasn't broken, the 'Robin Hood Gets Beat Up By A Girl' video was online.

'Rough night?' a familiar but unexpected voice asked.

The figure that stepped out of the dark was Diogo, a Portuguese biker and smuggler who'd looked after Robin and Marion when they went into hiding the previous summer. Diogo had taught Robin how to lift weights, how to swim better and how to look after boats. He was basically one of Robin's favourite people.

'Hey,' Robin said. He felt embarrassed and kept blinking, because he wondered if getting his head slammed into a metal container had scrambled his brain.

'What happened?' Diogo repeated, as he lent Robin an arm to help him walk.

'Brigand brats,' Robin said. 'Angry about me having gang colours and letting Marion get busted. To be honest, I mostly deserved it.'

'Feeling sorry for yourself and getting into a fight?' Diogo laughed as he gave Robin a friendly thump. 'You're a total cliché.'

Robin frowned. 'What are you on about?'

'Stupid fights are on page one in the *Teenage Boy Who Got Dumped* playbook.'

Robin scowled and sounded bitter. 'How does the entire world know I got dumped?'

'You have thousands of online fans who post rumours about you,' Diogo said. 'Though in my case, Emma Scarlock called and told me what was going on.'

'I'm baffled,' Robin admitted, as Diogo led him onto a steep downhill path towards the waterfront.

'You have a bounty on your head, and while the Brigands are scary, they're too disorganised to make reliable bodyguards. When my old friend Emma Scarlock found out you were heading to Lake Victoria, she asked if I'd be willing to tag along and keep an eye on you.'

Robin was torn. On one hand, he liked Diogo and was flattered that Emma Scarlock cared enough to protect him. On the other . . .

'I can look after myself,' Robin said crossly.

'I just picked you out of the dirt,' Diogo said.

Robin felt stupid. But he was too fond of Diogo to argue, and changed the subject.

'Does Cut-Throat mind you getting involved?' Robin asked.

Diogo shrugged as they kept walking. 'Me and Cut-Throat go way back. I've got boats, I know the Macondo River better than anyone. When I offered to come along, keep an eye on you and help solve his drone problem, he seemed very happy.'

'Where are we going?' Robin asked. 'Right now, I mean.'

'My boat,' Diogo said. 'I've got medicine that'll numb your pains and stop any swelling. There's even towels and hot water to clean up.'

Robin could only picture Diogo's open-hulled fan boat. '*Water Rat*?'

Diogo shook his head. 'Just bought another boat, *Dark Sky*.'

A muddy stretch of river and a bunch of moored boats came into view before Diogo needed to explain further. *Dark Sky* looked swanky in the light from the full moon. It was the kind of beefy powerboat that rich people buy, then sell cheaply when something new catches their eye.

'*Water Rat* suits shallow waters in the Delta,' Diogo explained, as he crossed the battered wooden jetty, then hopped onto his boat's rear deck. 'This boat is fast and comfortable for the thirty-hour cruise up to Lake Victoria. And since I just bought *Dark Sky*, it isn't red-flagged on any law enforcement smuggling database.'

Robin was wobbly after his battering, but nothing hurt badly as he grabbed a chrome handrail and stepped aboard.

'Plush,' Robin said, as he admired *Dark Sky*'s polished deck, then followed Diogo below.

There was a little galley and dining area with a dishwasher and fancy ovens, then a narrow corridor. The first door led to a master bedroom. Robin nosed through two more doors, one leading into a shower room and one to a utility space in the boat's bow, with four folding bunks and lots of random junk.

Diogo specialised in smuggling medical supplies to Forest People, so he had no problem finding pain meds and anti-inflammatories, while Robin used a monogrammed towel to wash his upper body and clean a couple of grazes.

'When do we leave?' Robin asked when he stepped out of the shower room.

'There are people here I want to see,' Diogo said. 'We'll leave around eight tomorrow morning.'

Robin's phone pinged as Diogo gave him four pills and a bottle of water. Matt Maid had sent a message with a link:

That girl crushed you!

Serves you right!

Best video EVER!!!!!!!!!!!!!!!!!!!!!!!!!!!!!!!!!!!!!

Robin clicked the link and saw that the video of himself getting battered had sixty thousand views in twenty minutes. The footage had been edited tightly, starting where the girl snatched Robin's wrist and ending with her boot getting wiped down his face.

'She's a little firecracker,' Diogo noted, as he watched over Robin's shoulder.

Robin slid onto a bench behind a fold-out galley table and buried his head in his arms. 'Does anyone even like me any more?' he moaned.

Diogo shrugged. 'For everyone like you who puts their neck on the line, there's a thousand sitting on their butts making snide remarks and trying to knock them down. What you've got to remember is: those people are sad losers.'

Robin looked up and smiled.

'Now stop sulking,' Diogo said, gesturing for Robin to stand up.

'Eh?' Robin said warily.

'I've got people to catch up with, and I'm not leaving you on this boat alone.'

'No,' Robin moaned. 'Can't I just flop on one of the bunks up front?'

'Robin Hood, I order you to stop feeling sorry for yourself and behave badly,' Diogo said, as he took a big breath. 'Dance, sneak a beer, try to snog a girl! Or kiss a boy for a change!'

'I refuse to enjoy myself,' Robin said, managing a half-smile, as Diogo gripped him under the arm and tugged him away from the table. 'Oww! My ribs still hurt.'

'Poor little snookums,' Diogo teased in a baby voice, as he made a half-serious attempt to put Robin in a headlock.

Robin dodged, but there wasn't far to go in *Dark Sky*'s galley. Diogo got one arm around Robin's thighs, then threw him effortlessly over his back.

'One mopey teen!' Diogo yelled as he stepped out onto the boat's rear deck with Robin dangling. 'He's been dumped, but we have the technology to make him bounce back!'

'Let me go, you knob!' Robin yelled, but he was also snorting with laughter. 'You're totally embarrassing.'

21. HAIR OF THE INCONTINENT DOG

Robin had several thoughts as he awoke the following morning.

My ribs hurt.

My head hurts more.

This bed smells revolting.

I have dog hair stuck to my face and . . .

'Morning, tiger!' Diogo said cheerfully, as he gave Robin a poke with a burnt stick. 'You have fun last night?'

Robin sat up, shielding his eyes from early sun coming through a skylight. His tracksuit bottoms were ripped, he'd slept in a large dog basket, there was no sign of his T-shirt, and he had a phone number written down his arm in black marker pen.

Memories of the previous night were a mix of blurry, horrifying and hilarious.

Diving into a mosh pit near the bonfire.

Women getting me to autograph their T-shirts.

Running when drunk Brigands started blasting shotguns and throwing axes.

Bumping into the girl who beat me up and . . . EWW!

Snogging the girl who beat me up.

Puking.

'I dropped by Cut-Throat's trailer and grabbed your backpack and archery gear,' Diogo said. Robin looked around and found his boots amidst bodies flopped over beds and sofas. 'You can scrub up when we get to the boat.'

Robin looked down at his mud-caked tracksuit bottoms and saw a damp patch. 'I *can't* have wet myself.'

Diogo smirked. 'I suspect the basket you slept in belongs to an old dog. One that no longer has control of their bodily functions.'

Robin looked down at himself and gawped in horror. 'I slept in dog pee!'

Diogo laughed, but a bare-assed Brigand on the bed at the opposite end of the container didn't.

'Lemme sleep,' he growled, then flicked a half-drunk beer can at Diogo.

Robin found his shirt and phone and stepped carefully over the sleeping bodies. As he exited into a chilly spring morning, the sun felt like lasers drilling his skull.

'I swear someone spiked my drink.' Robin groaned as Diogo led the way towards his boat. 'Beer tastes disgusting, so I drank *one* can of this pineapple cocktail thing before switching to Coke . . .'

'Those alcopop things can be deadly,' Diogo said. 'They taste sweet, but most are stronger than beer. And it probably didn't sit well with all the food you ate.'

'The barbecue was amazing,' Robin said, though just thinking about it now made him queasy.

'I kept an eye out to make sure you didn't drink any more. And you've got to admit, you forgot your troubles and enjoyed yourself.'

'It was mad fun,' Robin admitted. 'Until the puking.'

'If you talk to Emma, Indio or Karma, maybe don't mention that I encouraged you to let your hair down.'

'Corrupting an innocent boy who was happy to stay on your boat and fall asleep,' Robin teased, before Diogo changed the subject.

'Any bounty hunter with a brain cell can work out where you are in that video of Brigand kids beating you up,' Diogo said. 'We need to leave ASAP.'

'What about Cut-Throat?' Robin asked.

Diogo scoffed. 'It'll be afternoon before that lump wakes. He'll drive and meet us at Lake Victoria.'

As they approached the water, Robin stepped over smashed beer and gin bottles. He was amused by the sight of several Brigands passed out on the pontoon, then shocked when he saw a little speedboat that had clearly caught fire after getting wrecked on rocks twenty metres from shore.

'Was anyone hurt?' Robin asked.

Diogo laughed. 'Woman bumped her head and one guy's beard caught fire, but they just waded back to shore.'

Robin laughed as he stepped onto *Dark Sky* behind Diogo, then opened the sliding door to go below deck.

'No, no, no!' Diogo said. 'Your cologne is dog urine, and no way are you traipsing mud through my new boat.'

'But I need a shower.'

Diogo pointed to the front of the boat. 'Use the deck hose.'

'That'll be freezing.'

'Character-building,' Diogo said, as he cracked a huge smile. 'I'll fetch a bar of soap.'

22. FIFTEEN-MINUTE BREAK

The nurse who came on shift at 7am had a woman in agony with kidney stones, another coming out of surgery with sixty stitches from a knife wound and no bed to put them in. After checking Marion's vitals and looking at the tiny graze down her arm, her verdict was blunt.

'I don't know how you ended up here, inmate. I've got *real* patients to deal with.'

The biker who was supposed to call Stable Block and tell them to send a guard and pick Marion up claimed nobody was answering the phone and made sure Marion got a cooked breakfast.

But by nine, Marion's comfy bed was a memory. She'd changed into a laundered set of prison uniform and a sergeant she'd never seen before was bawling at her for losing a shoe.

'Don't think I'm taking you down to stores to get a new one, I've got better things to do.'

Marion started walking in one shoe, but it felt weird so she went barefoot.

'My surgeon said I'm supposed to wear a foam brace on my leg for another two weeks,' Marion said.

'Do I look like someone who gives a damn?' the sergeant asked, before shoving Marion. 'Move out.'

The prison's bare concrete floors were crumbling and Marion trod carefully to avoid lumps that might cut her foot. After a couple of long hallways and an elevator ride, Marion realised she was being taken to meat processing for work, but the sergeant didn't take Marion through her usual entrance.

'I work around the other side, with the mixers,' Marion said, assuming the guard had made a mistake.

'You did,' the man said. 'But we have punishment details for people who attack guards with stun sticks.'

A blast of cold hit Marion as the sergeant unlocked a bright yellow door. After passing through a curtain of plastic insulation strips, Marion saw that she was in a chilled warehouse, with inmates driving forklifts. The floor was so cold, it stung her bare feet.

The warehouse was neat, modern and covered in safety warnings. Huge metal racks rose fifteen metres and were stacked with boxes of frozen burgers, meatballs and all the other stuff produced in the factory next door.

'Is this our new miscreant?' a thuggish supervisor said, as he wandered across. He wore an insulated suit and thick gloves as he stared at Marion, barefoot and shivering in shorts. 'Not much of her.'

'Enough of her to use a stun stick on one of my colleagues,' the sergeant explained. 'I want her on twelve-hour shifts, and make sure she works hard.'

The supervisor looked wary. 'Even on punishment, juveniles can only work six.'

The sergeant smirked as she handed the supervisor a crumpled pink form. 'As you can see, Marion is twenty years old. She can work full shifts.'

'I'm thirteen,' Marion protested. 'This is—'

Before Marion could say 'crap', the guard grabbed a handful of her hair and yanked it to snap her head back.

'Inmate, you are a fifty-year-old pink elephant if I say you are. If you wish to disagree, you can discuss it with the end of my boot. Is that clear?'

'Yes, boss,' Marion answered as her face twisted in pain.

The sergeant let Marion go, then gave her a shove that sent her sprawling over the cold floor.

'My name is Mr Marez, but you will call me sir,' the supervisor said, as the sergeant headed off. 'Clear?'

'Yes, sir,' Marion said, as she stood up.

'You will take boots, gloves and an insulated suit from the row of hooks on the back wall. Dress quickly, then I will assign you a tablet and a hand trolley. The tablet will tell you which items to take from which shelves and which container to bring them to.

'You must walk briskly, but never run. You will not obstruct forklift trucks. You will get one fifteen-minute break every three hours. I don't care if your back hurts, your arms ache, or your fingers are numb from cold. If you stop work, you'd better be dead.

'If you're slow, you will lose your break. If you drop a box or cause any other damages, you will lose your break. If you lose all of your breaks, you'll spend the night in a punishment cell. Clear?'

'OK, sir,' Marion said sourly.

Marez poked Marion in the chest. 'Use that tone again and you'll lose your break,' he warned. 'Now snap to it!'

23. THE GOLDEN ROBE

Robin didn't enjoy the icy shower, especially when Diogo fired up *Dark Sky*'s twin turbines and sent him sprawling half-naked across the bow deck. But the cold cleared Robin's head and he felt alive, watching the wall of spray thrown up around *Dark Sky*'s bow.

As Diogo piloted the boat through the shallow tributary, keeping a careful eye on his depth sounder and radar, Robin stepped into clean underwear, hosed his muddy boots, then decided that tracksuit bottoms with dog pee were too gross and kicked them over the side.

He went inside to clean his teeth, check his bruises and finish getting dressed. He found a thick bathrobe with gold piping in a cabinet and couldn't resist putting it on, though it was crazy big and brushed against the floor.

'Look at Mr Fancy Pants,' Diogo said, booming with laughter as Robin emerged onto the rear deck.

Dark Sky had reached the Macondo River proper. Huge trees craned over either embankment and Robin pulled up the robe's hood, because a little ferry boat rammed with Forest People was coming the other way.

'Where are they off to?' Robin asked.

'That's Yashvir's boat,' Diogo said, as he gave the ferry captain a wave. 'They'll be heading south for sweatshop work, or farm labour.'

Once the ferry passed, Robin admired the sun catching the river and water birds feeding along the embankments.

'Want to see how fast my baby can go?' Diogo asked, as he tapped the radar screen. 'There's no boats nearby.'

Robin grinned as Diogo let him sit in the quilted leather captain's chair and guided his hand to the twin throttle levers. In front were beautiful, chromed gauges and touchscreens showing navigation, underwater sonar and radar.

'It's like a luxury car,' Robin noted.

Diogo smiled at the compliment and gave Robin an order. 'Gun it!'

Robin pushed the throttle levers forward and was shocked by the din of two powerful jet turbines. *Dark Sky*'s nose lifted out of the water and the acceleration kicked Robin back in his seat.

'This is awesome!' Robin said, as an automatic wiper cleared spray from the screen in front of him.

As *Dark Sky* sped up the ride grew bumpier, making Robin aware of his headache and his phone sliding from the pocket of his white robe.

When the big chrome dial in the centre of the console showed fifty-five knots, Diogo tapped Robin's throttle hand and made him pull back.

'Fifty-five is about a hundred kilometres per hour,' Diogo shouted, as the engine whoosh became less deafening. 'But you can't keep that up for long because turbines guzzle fuel.'

'That was mega!' Robin said, though now they'd slowed down he looked behind and felt sorry for the birds who'd been disturbed by their wake.

Robin stayed at the helm, cruising at a gentler twelve knots, while Diogo went inside to cook scrambled eggs with peppers and hot sauce for breakfast.

'Chilli kick for your hangover!' Diogo explained when he brought out the food.

As the big Portuguese took back the captain's chair, Robin settled on the wraparound sofa at the boat's rear. He ate his eggs, toast and juice at a fold-out table, then checked his phone to see if the Super had found anything interesting since yesterday.

But Robin couldn't log in. He thought it was because there was no signal, but websites worked so he decided the Super must have crashed.

It wasn't a major problem. The Super used cutting-edge software developed by the online retailer TwoTu, and it occasionally broke. But awkwardly, only one person at Sherwood Castle knew how to reboot the system and restore searches that were running before it crashed.

It was a Saturday, so she wasn't in school. She answered on the third ring.

'Hey, party boy, how's the hangover?' Josie said, cheerful, but a touch wary.

'What makes you think I have a hangover?'

'You're kidding!' Josie snorted. 'There's online video where you're dancing on top of a shipping container with half-naked women and you look *completely* wasted.'

'I had *one* pineapple alcopop, which was vile.'

'Sure,' Josie scoffed. 'Karma wasn't impressed when Matt showed her.'

'He's such a stirrer.' Robin groaned. 'Did you see the other video?'

'Getting your ass kicked had three million views when I looked.'

'Once I leave the castle, I've got zero privacy,' Robin complained. 'I *hate* everyone knowing my business.'

'Such irony,' Josie snorted.

'What irony?' Robin asked.

'You use the Super to access *thousands* of stolen databases and invade the privacy of half the planet. But you moan because some drunk biker posts video of you dancing.'

Robin looked up as Diogo piloted *Dark Sky* beneath an iron bridge. 'Speaking of the Super, I called because it needs a reset and restore.'

'I was planning to spend my Saturday scoffing M&M's and watching sitcoms,' Josie said. 'But I *suppose* I could squeeze in a trip to the Nest. If you like, I could even go through search results.'

'That could be useful,' Robin agreed. 'Do you know what you're looking for?'

'Corrupt prison guards, operational details, ways to smuggle stuff into Pelican Island, or bust Marion out.'

Robin laughed. 'We're hoping to get Marion a phone so we can talk to her, but the last person to escape from Pelican Island without drowning was a German fighter pilot during World War Two.'

'You can't be sure if you don't look,' Josie said airily. 'I'll blast a message when the Super's running again.'

'Later potato,' Robin said, before hanging up.

As Robin rested his phone in his lap he saw an eight per cent battery warning, then realised he'd had a normal conversation with Josie. It still hurt when he thought about getting dumped, but now it was more of a dull ache than an elephant crushing his chest.

'That your ex?' Diogo asked, as he looked back from the captain's chair. 'Everything OK?'

'I'll survive,' Robin said, as he grabbed his empty mug and breakfast plate. 'I'm going in. My phone needs charging, plus it's breezy and there's not much under this robe.'

'And you look an idiot,' Diogo pointed out.

Robin cheekily flipped his friend off as he walked inside.

24. WORLD'S BIGGEST BATHTUB

They reached the colossal dam at Darley Dale just before eleven. Diogo steered his boat into a broad canal, through huge hydraulically powered gates, then tied *Dark Sky* up in the first of three ship elevators that would take them a hundred and fifty metres to the top of the dam.

By the time the gates closed, the lock held a dozen boats. Diogo seemed to know everyone on the river. As the tightly packed vessels were lifted to the next stretch of canal, he hopped over to an unladen timber barge and lunched on hot dogs with lively captains and crew.

It was safest for Robin to stay out of sight, so he crashed on Diogo's bed in the master suite, catching up on sleep, then got his schoolbooks out of his bag and drew graphs for the dreaded science project.

When homework became unbearably dull,[1] Robin

---

[1] After twelve minutes . . .

opened his phone and watched online clips from the night before. The video of him getting battered was an embarrassment and had drawn tonnes of comments from haters, but there were loads of clips of Robin behaving badly at the party that most people found funny or cool.

The biggest boost to Robin's ego came from comedian Darrell Snubs. He'd got half a million likes by reposting the video of Robin dancing on top of the shipping container with the comment:

```
My pal Robin showing how it's done!
No. 1 PARTY animal.
```

It was two when *Dark Sky* exited the final ship elevator into the vast lake behind the dam. It was the perfect space to hit the speedboat's seventy-knot top speed, except the lake had a fifteen-knot limit and Diogo was keen to avoid attention from the river police.

Dark Sky was still faster than the other boats leaving the lock, though, and once they had gained some distance, Robin came out for fresh air.

The dimensions of Darley Dale's ship elevators prevented anything bigger than a logging barge getting this far upriver. In decades past, this beautiful stretch of the Macondo would have buzzed with pleasure craft on a bright spring Saturday. But widespread fear of Forest People and the more realistic threat of bandits meant the guest houses and eateries that once lined this section of river had rotted away, or become homes for refugees.

Robin was sick of being on the boat when the sun set and hundreds of flying midges decided to attack. It was dark as Diogo cruised up to Fuel N Food, one of the few riverside businesses still trading. There were several customer boats tied to the wooden pontoons out front and a dazzling neon sign that reflected across the water.

'We're almost out of gas,' Diogo told Robin as they pulled in. 'The diner can be rough, so stay below till I've looked around.'

There was zero chance cops or rangers would venture this deep into the forest, so Fuel N Food provided its own security. The guard by the entrance held a machine gun, and a sign above read:

Fuel N Food reserves the right to shoot customers who don't pay.

'Nice boat,' the guard told Diogo, as she kissed him on both cheeks. 'You win the lottery?'

'Got a great deal,' Diogo said. 'Can you get her filled with the high-octane stuff?'

Robin peeked out from *Dark Sky*'s galley as Diogo went into the diner, then ducked as a guy who looked a hundred years old came along the pontoon dragging a fuel hose. A moment later Diogo came out, shook the refuelling guy's hand then gestured to Robin.

'There's a booth up back where we'll be out of sight,' Diogo said. 'I've known the owners for years. The food won't win awards, but it'll fill you up.'

25. CALAMARI AND SWITCHBLADES

Robin put on a baseball cap and hurried across the pontoon in the dark. It was good to get off the boat and stretch his legs, but the inside of Food N Fuel made him feel like he was in some old cowboy movie.

There was a greasy kitchen up back, a TV showing Russian ping-pong and a dimly lit side room where four women and two men sat around a poker table piled with cash.

Robin ordered fish and chips, flicked ants off the table while he waited, and smiled when a huge cod and chips arrived, along with Diogo's steak and some battered shrimp and calamari that they hadn't ordered.

'For a special young man,' the waiter said, as he gave Robin a wink. 'Extra seafood, on the house.'

'Thanks,' Robin said, as the first crispy batter shattered in his mouth. 'It looks great.'

They'd almost cleared their plates when two red-headed brothers tied a little cargo boat to the pontoon and came inside. Nothing about them drew attention, but when the shorter brother spotted Diogo, he puffed his chest and charged over.

'You owe me six thousand, you dirty Spaniard,' the guy began.

Diogo looked up with contempt. 'I'm Portuguese,' he growled.

'Healthcare pass you sold me was junk. My sister went to hospital eight months pregnant, got arrested and deported when her baby was born. My brother-in-law was so angry he stabbed me.' The guy lifted up his T-shirt and Robin saw a recently stitched scar across his tummy. Diogo stood up to face off against the furious guy, while the guard came inside and the poker game froze.

'I told you health cards aren't my line of business,' Diogo began. He sounded a lot more foreign when he was angry. 'I said I knew a woman who could get fake healthcare documents, but that I couldn't vouch for her.'

'You're full of crap,' the little guy roared. 'Six thousand was my life savings, and my sister had her baby on the floor of a filthy detention camp.'

Robin backed further into the booth, pulled down his cap to hide his face and wished he hadn't left his bow aboard *Dark Sky*.

'I told you it was risky!' Diogo shouted. 'I'm sorry it didn't work out.'

'Least you can do is give our six thousand back,' the taller brother said, as he thumped on the table.

'Smuggling is what I know,' Diogo answered, holding up his hands. 'Shouldn't have got involved, but you seemed desperate.'

'Fancy boat must have cost plenty,' the taller guy said snarkily. 'How many others did you rip off to get that?'

As the guy said this, the shorter one pulled a switchblade and lunged at Diogo. The tight booth gave the big biker nowhere to back up. As Diogo tried to get the attacker's arm, Robin grabbed what was left of his dinner and smashed his plate over the guy's head.

As chips flew through the air, the attacker stumbled back and Diogo yelped because the blade had slashed his knuckles as he tried to defend himself. As the taller brother threw a punch at Diogo, the little one, who wasn't happy about having a plate cracked over his head, went for Robin.

Being wedged in the booth made it hard to escape. Robin sprayed ketchup in his attacker's face, then scrambled onto the tabletop.

'We don't have fighting here!' the guard yelled. As she closed in with the machine gun, Food N Fuel's owner picked a shotgun from a rack behind the kitchen counter. Robin feared getting shot, but as Diogo and the tall brother traded punches on the floor the shorter one tried to slash Robin's leg.

Robin grabbed the metal pendant lamp over the table. He lifted his legs, imagining that he'd swing forward and kick his opponent in the face. But light fittings aren't designed to hold the weight of a teenager and the wire tore out of the ceiling fixture, bringing down chunks of ceiling and fusing the restaurant's electrics.

As the diner plunged into darkness, Robin managed to knock his attacker off with a kick. But he landed hard on the tabletop, with a fork sticking in his bum and chunks of plaster landing on his head.

The short guy went for Robin again, but now the guard stepped in. 'Knife down or I'll blow your brains out!' she warned.

As the guard made the short guy retreat, the owner knocked the taller brother away from Diogo by bashing him with the wooden stock of his shotgun. Robin thought the owner would be annoyed because he'd torn up the ceiling and fused the electrics, but he helped Robin slide off the table.

'He took our life savings for a useless piece of plastic,' the tall guy protested to the guard desperately. 'Why take his side?'

Robin wondered this too, but the guard gave the tall guy a vicious boot in the stomach before answering.

'Diogo smuggles medicine for Forest People when he could get rich bringing guns or drugs,' the guard spat, then drummed a finger on her chest. 'I *personally* know people Diogo has helped when they were sick and couldn't afford medicine. And hundreds more along this river will say the same.'

A 'Yes!' and a shout of 'That's right!' came from the group at the poker table, while someone out back reset a fuse to get the power back.

Robin just had four little dots of blood where the fork dug in, but the cut across Diogo's knuckles was deeper. As the biker wrapped a grubby dishcloth around his hand to stop the bleeding, the guard dragged the red-headed brothers across the floor and made them sit against the counter.

The guard looked at Diogo. 'Want me to take 'em out back and break their legs?'

Robin hoped the guard was joking, though she seemed like the type who'd enjoy some brutality. Diogo took a deep breath as he took a money clip from his jeans with his good hand, then awkwardly used the bloody one to peel off four hundred pounds.

'That should cover food, fuel, damage. Plus, dinner for the two gents on the floor,' Diogo said, as he gave the battered redheads a pitying look.

'No way,' the owner said, trying to hand Diogo back the money. 'I won't feed pigs who attack you.'

Diogo pointed out at *Dark Sky* and spoke wisely. 'It'll take 'em a while to eat. I'll get half an hour's start and their little boat won't catch me.'

'I'll make sure they don't come after you,' the guard said menacingly, while the owner tucked the four hundred into Diogo's shirt pocket.

'You're like family, Diogo,' the owner said, then winked at Robin. 'And wherever you're going next, be sure to look after this guy.'

26. EXTRA-SPICY BEANS

In almost fourteen years on Earth, Marion Maid had broken her shoulder falling out of a tree, taken pellets from a bandit's shotgun, had giant rocks lobbed at her head by Matt, burned the skin off her hand on a hotplate and survived three painful surgeries on her club foot.

On the face of it, working in a warehouse wasn't so bad. But after six hours she was in the worst pain of her life. Her muscles hurt from lifting huge boxes of frozen food, her whole body was numb from cold, and clomping adult-sized safety boots had blistered her feet.

Worst of all, if anyone messed up and caused an outgoing container to be delayed, everyone lost their break. And since it was Marion's first day, she messed up a lot. One scary male inmate slammed her into a wall when she fetched the wrong box of burgers and another spat on her for being too slow.

After twelve hours, Marion got back to Stable Block, holding her single shoe, her heel and toes bleeding, so tired she was scared she'd fall if she let her eyes close.

If prisoners worked through mealtimes, a metal food tray was left on a rack in Stable Block's dining area. Marion was desperate to sleep, but hungry too.

The other prisoners were already locked down for the night, so she was alone as she grabbed the meal tray. She wanted to cry as she looked at her dinner: a carton of apple juice, congealed baked beans, cold mash and a splat of green veg. The best bit of prison dinner was always the slice of cake or pudding cup, but someone had stolen it.

As Marion slumped on a bench at a metal table and pushed the straw into her apple juice, a clanking side gate opened and Danielle bounced in.

'Inmate, you stink,' Danielle sneered, as she pinched her nose like a four-year-old. 'You're gonna get ripe, coming back here every day when showers are closed. Eating dinner cold. Pity Daddy's biker friends couldn't keep you in hospital.'

Marion sucked juice as the guard took out her phone then sat astride the metal bench.

'Your old partner has been having fun,' Danielle taunted, as she showed Marion a video of Robin partying. 'Dancing, drinking, girls. Teenage years are a blast . . . for some.'

Marion grudgingly turned her head and saw Robin lit by flames from a huge bonfire as he boogied madly on top of a shipping container. He'd grown a few centimetres and grinned like his life was perfect.

'Then there's poor old Marion,' Danielle said, before sighing theatrically. 'Working twelve hours a day, six days a week. Humping twenty-kilo meat packs in freezing cold.'

Marion was determined not to cry in front of Danielle. 'Let me guess,' Marion said as she narrowed her eyes. 'If I do what you want and grass my friends, everything will be fabulous.'

Danielle shrugged. 'You'll still be in here, inmate. But you'll be back to six-hour shifts with the mixers and I'll make sure Mafia 13 keep their hands off you.'

Marion almost gagged on a scoop of cold beans.

'You've been on duty all day,' Marion told the guard thoughtfully. 'You've had time to speak to Freya and my other cellmates. If any of them signed a statement, you wouldn't be wasting time talking to me.'

'Watch your tone, inmate,' Danielle snapped.

Marion sensed a raw nerve and kept going. 'Guess you'll have to fill all those forms and explain to your bosses how there was a mini-riot in Stable Block and nobody to pin the blame on.'

Danielle swelled with anger and hissed, 'I can crush you like a bug.'

'As a juvenile inmate,' Marion continued, 'I'm not supposed to work – or be educated, since that's what you call it – for more than six hours per day. As a female,

I'm not supposed to work with male prisoners. Even if you cut my outside phone calls and visiting rights, I can get another inmate to contact my Aunt Lucy. She's not wanted by the cops, so she visits me every month and can file a complaint.'

'Sure,' Danielle said, as she pointed at Marion's bloody feet. 'But external complaints take six weeks to process and you're wrecked after one shift.'

Marion felt crushed thinking about her options: suffer weeks of misery in the warehouse, or write a statement full of lies that would mean her closest friends got years added to their sentences.

'Eat up then,' Danielle said. 'I want you back in your cell in three minutes.' As the beefy guard stood up, she studied Marion's food tray. 'Looks a little bland,' she said, as she pulled her pepper spray off her belt. 'Allow me to zing it up for you.'

Marion thrust herself quickly down the bench as Danielle nuked her tray with strings of gluey pepper spray. Just getting near the stuff made eyes sting, so there was no way Marion could eat it.

'If you don't like spice,' Danielle said, smiling nastily as she backed towards the exit, 'then you'll be a *very* hungry girl by morning . . .'

27. DAMNED FINE PIE

Diogo spent two hours putting space between himself and the brothers who'd attacked him at Food N Fuel. It was near midnight and Robin was asleep below deck when Diogo set anchor a few metres from the riverbank, activated motion alarms on deck and crashed out in the master bedroom.

But the wound across Diogo's knuckles was painful and he tormented himself, imagining how a large group of forest bandits could climb aboard and seize his expensive new boat. When sleep seemed hopeless, Diogo rebandaged his hand, made a sandwich, then upped anchor and began an eight-knot moonlit cruise.

There were clouds and drizzle as the sun rose and the river broadened from a hundred metres to more than two kilometres as it merged into the vast open water of Lake Victoria.

'Come look!' Diogo shouted when he heard Robin flush the toilet.

The teenager stumbled on deck, barefoot and sleepy-eyed as misty rain swirled on the wind.

'Did you sleep?' Robin asked when he realised how far they'd gone.

The thought made Diogo stretch into a yawn. 'Barely,' he admitted. 'How was your bunk?'

'Not great, but I slept solid,' Robin said, as he rubbed his ribs, bruised thanks to the girl who'd battered him. 'Did you drug me again?'

As Diogo laughed, Robin peered through rain on the windshield and saw an island near the lake's centre. Its outline of brick towers was familiar from movies and documentaries about the country's most notorious prison.

'Pelican Island,' Robin said, getting a weird vibe as he remembered that Marion was on there somewhere.

'We'll cruise in for a look,' Diogo said. 'There's a hundred-metre exclusion zone. But pleasure boats and tours cruise around the prison, so nobody will pay attention to us.'

Robin looked surprised. 'Tourists?'

Diogo nodded. 'The river east of Lake Victoria is bandit country, but most of the lakefront is safe and the western edge is well posh. Villas, marinas and restaurants.'

'We'll fit in with this boat,' Robin noted.

It was the weekend, so despite dull weather there were sail boats and jet skis on the water as they neared the centre of the lake, which was thirty kilometres long and twenty across at its widest point. Robin cooked bacon and eggs and brewed Diogo's morning coffee. By the time they'd eaten, Pelican Island loomed large.

The water around the prison was choppy, and warning buoys with blinking amber lights marked the exclusion zone. Huge yellow billboards warned boats not to rescue swimmers who might be escapees and said they could be shot at for entering the exclusion zone. But heavy graffiti on the island's sandstone cliffs suggested these signs were a bluff.

'There's binoculars in the cabinet above the microwave,' Diogo said.

As Robin came out with the binoculars strapped around his neck, he hid his face because a double-deck tourist boat was chugging by. Fortunately, passengers' eyes and smartphone cameras were all fixed on the intimidating walls and rusty bars of Central's ten-storey tower.

Robin could hear a tinny commentary from the tour boat speakers. 'When prisoners were first sent to Pelican Island in 1707, they lived in wooden huts and were made to work mining guano that had been deposited over thousands of years by the vast bird colony from which the island gets its name.

'Today just one small pelican colony remains at the island's eastern tip, but more than five thousand inmates live here. Despite complaints that the island prison is outdated and expensive to maintain, the current government has no plans to shut it down.'

The commentary got drowned out as Diogo powered up *Dark Sky*'s engines to get away from the tour boat.

Robin swung the powerful binoculars up and saw enough detail to read ID numbers on the uniform of armed guards. He also studied the helicopter on Central's roof and prisoners staring through wire at the edge of a rooftop exercise yard.

But Robin's real interest was locating the drone detectors. The diagrams on Castillo Defence Systems' website showed the detectors as circular black devices. They were powered by small solar panels, with parabolic dishes to capture sound from a distance and sophisticated microphone arrays in the centre.

The choppy water made it hard to scan with the binoculars, and while Robin was amused to see a giant green **ROBIN HOOD LIVES** amidst the graffiti, his frustration grew until he got blinded by sun reflecting off a small solar panel.

'Think I've found one,' Robin told Diogo triumphantly. He snapped a picture of the location with his phone. It was ten metres up, over a patch of shingle beach and by aged graffiti that read **FREE THE COVENTRY FOUR**.

'How many detectors are you expecting?' Diogo asked.

'Ten to fifteen for the whole island,' Robin guessed. 'But we shouldn't need to disable all of them.'

After finding the first detector, Robin realised he could abandon the binoculars and look for reflections coming off the solar panels. He quickly located two more detectors, and seven before Diogo decided they'd been circling the island for too long.

'We'll go meet Ollie,' Diogo said, pushing the throttles forward and steering away from the prison. 'See what they've got to say.'

While the western banks of Lake Victoria were posh and the east bordered on bandit country, South Bank was somewhere between the two. It had a reputation for housing wealthy dropouts and creative types. Many of them lived in eccentric houseboats or wooden pole houses that hung over the water.

'Cut-Throat said it's a black canal boat, with chromed bike wheels decorating the sides,' Diogo told Robin as South Bank drew near.

Robin assumed the boat would stand out, but as *Dark Sky* cruised along South Bank, he marvelled at houseboats designed to look like sharks, a rusting US Navy minesweeper, river barges converted into vegetable plots, a parrot-stuffed aviary and a three-storey pole house draped in shimmering gold fabric.

Diogo eventually spotted Ollie's houseboat on an inlet close to a boatyard.

'Ahoy, mateys!' Ollie shouted, as *Dark Sky* pulled alongside.

At first glance, Ollie looked like the Brigand they had once been. But they'd abandoned the macho biker world, shaved their beard and swapped their grimy jeans for a red dress and stockings.

'It's been too long,' Diogo said fondly as he hopped onto the houseboat and hugged Ollie. 'You look well.'

'Love the new boat,' Ollie said, then looked at Robin, who was tying *Dark Sky* to the houseboat. 'And you're the famous kid! I've been looking forward to meeting you!'

Ollie swept Robin into a hug as he stepped onto the houseboat. 'I have a Robin Hood sweatshirt for you to autograph for my nephew, if that's OK?'

'No problem,' Robin agreed.

'The lady two boats across gave me an apple pie for servicing her heat pump,' Ollie said, as they led the way inside the boat. 'Her pastry is to die for, and I'll make a pot of tea.'

'Can't go wrong with pie,' Robin said keenly as he took in Ollie's home.

It was a twenty-five-metre broad-beam canal boat, so there was tonnes of space. One end had a lounge and kitchen while the rear was a workshop stacked with old appliances, from ancient tellies to water pumps and air fryers.

As Diogo squatted down to stroke Ollie's pit bull, Robin's eyes were drawn to a shelf lined with drones and battery packs. They were Ishtar T7s. A solid, basic drone that was big enough to carry contraband, but cheap enough for the owner not to lose sleep if it crashed into the lake or got blasted by prison guards.

'Is this what you've been using?' Robin asked, as he looked at the drones' mangled propellers and scraped underbodies. 'Looks like they've made a few trips.'

Ollie nodded. 'I had seven drones, but only two still fly, and I daren't take them near Pelican Island.'

'Have you tried disconnecting the GPS receiver and flying full manual?' Robin asked.

Ollie laughed and pointed at the mountain of appliances. 'I can fix motorbikes, fridges, ovens, clocks or anything else mechanical. But computers and software turn my brain to mush.'

'There's a few things we can try,' Robin said. 'Though I have a nasty feeling we'll have to get close to Pelican Island and take the detectors out.'

'It's great that you're eager,' Ollie told Robin. 'But Cut-Throat's not even here yet. So, let's start with apple pie and see where we go from there.'

28. WE ARE THE MODS

Diogo and Ollie were old friends with a lot in common. Fanatical bikers in their teens, both had rejected the gang lifestyle and started a new life on the water. After one mug of tea, they switched to rum and told stories from their glorious past. Meanwhile, Robin tinkered with one of Ollie's drones.

Robin thought he might be able to defeat Pelican Island's drone defences if he changed how the drone worked. A web search led him to a hobbyist forum where lots of people had posted questions about Ishtar T7 drones, and Robin found posts talking about the drone's engineering mode.

After downloading a small program and connecting the T7 to his laptop, Robin was able to access lots of extra settings which were meant for repair technicians. The most important was the ability to turn off the drone's geofencing system. This was a legal requirement for all drones, and prevented them from flying over restricted areas like airports and military bases.

Robin also turned off the location beacon. This made the drone easier to find if it crashed or got lost, but also made it easier to detect. Lastly, he found a forum post where a group of birdwatchers spoke about ways to make their T7s quieter by using bigger propellers, fitting rubber gaskets around the motors and making motors run at a lower speed in flight.

'It makes the drone slower and reduces flight time,' Robin explained to Ollie. 'But the defence system works by detecting sound then jamming control signals. If we fly quiet, we might be able to sneak in undetected.'

Ollie had a tonne of parts from broken or crashed drones. They found some larger propellers, while the rubber suspension from an old record player provided ideal material to wrap around the motors.

The lake was busy with pleasure craft and Ollie didn't want people to witness drones taking off from their boat, so they drove Ollie's rust bucket Renault a few kilometres east to a stretch of deserted lakefront.

The pair walked out onto a wobbly jetty that had been engulfed in tall reeds. Robin put on a set of first-person-view goggles as Ollie switched on the drone. After launching, Robin took the drone up fifty metres and practised basic manoeuvres, like forwards, backwards, hovering, then he skimmed the drone a couple of metres above the choppy lake water.

'How's it feel?' Ollie asked.

'Sluggish,' Robin said. 'I'm used to flying a stealth drone that's smaller and more powerful.'

'It's a lot quieter than before the modifications,' Ollie said. 'Bring her in to land, then you can take a run at the prison.'

The drone's software was confused by the big propellers and slower motors. Even though they had landing assist turned on, a strong gust almost flipped the T7 into the lake as Robin brought it down.

Ollie opened the belly of the drone and clipped in a fresh battery pack. After launch, it took the drone four minutes to skim the four and a half kilometres of water between the lakeside and Pelican Island.

Robin flew low to minimise the chances of being seen, but had to swerve to avoid a water skier.

The plan was to steer between the drone detectors he'd spotted earlier, so Robin targeted a flat section of sandstone cliff that someone had sprayed with a huge **GRIM819** tag.

As the drone skimmed past a flashing buoy, Robin pulled up to gain height and was momentarily thrown off-kilter as the drone missed a seagull by less than a metre.

'I've not got a T7 this close to the wall since the defence went up,' Ollie said hopefully as they watched Robin's first-person-view on their phone. 'Your mods might be working.'

The drone shot up the sandstone cliffs, then over a huge wall topped with searchlights and lines of razor wire.

Robin levelled out and caught a view across the rusting metal roof of an industrial building, but as he nudged the drone to fly inside prison walls the image froze.

'Tits!' Robin gasped.

His screen went black. Then he got a couple of seconds of glitchy video where the T7 spun out of control.

'They got us,' Ollie growled, as Robin took off the FPV goggles and sighed.

'Well, that didn't work,' Robin said dejectedly as he hopped off the jetty. 'But it was worth a try.'

29. THE GODMOTHER

They stopped at a lakeside farmers market on the drive back. As Ollie joined an epic queue at a stall selling fresh bread, Robin kept low in the back of the Renault and picked up a call from Josie.

''Sup, dirtbag,' Josie began cheerfully. 'How's Lake Victoria?'

'Big,' Robin said, as a double buggy rolled by the car. 'How's our research going?'

'It's going,' Josie said. 'I've been looking at the Pelican Island staff's financial records, and so many look dodgy. I've found at least ten staff who have so much money that they *must* be corrupt.

'None of them are stupid enough to wear designer suits or drive around in a Ferrari, but if you scratch the surface, you've got guards who own fancy holiday homes, guards setting up businesses and playing the stock market. And Alan dug up something even more suspicious.'

Robin baulked as he jealously imagined his former best friend in the Nest snogging Josie.

'Him!' Robin grunted.

Josie was unrepentant. 'The Super has generated a zillion leads. Alan was here at the Nest all last night, helping me sift data.'

'So, what did he find?' Robin asked grudgingly.

'An employee called Jay Patel,' Josie explained. 'Patel was employed to work as a teacher in the prison's Arts and Crafts programme two months before the drone defence system was installed. His only qualifications are a grade 4 GCSE in Food Technology and the fact that his godmother is Anne Kemp—'

Robin interrupted. 'I already looked into Kemp. She's deputy warden for the whole prison. She has two hundred grand stashed with a Turkish bank and flies first class when she goes on holiday.'

'She's also in charge of security for the entire prison,' Josie added.

'Bikers used drones to smuggle stuff into the prison,' Robin said thoughtfully. 'Then Anne Kemp orders a system to stop the drones, and at the same time, employs her unqualified godson to teach Arts and Crafts.'

'I bet an Arts and Crafts teacher could bring in all kinds of paints and supplies,' Josie said. 'And staff must get searched, but what minimum wage prison guard would want to stick their arm in a tin of paint, or slice up a tube of glue?'

'Especially when you're searching the deputy warden's godson,' Robin agreed. 'Cut-Throat said it felt like everything was in place to take over the bikers' smuggling operation on the day drone defence got switched on. So your facts fit perfectly.'

'But it gets worse,' Josie said. 'Since biker gangs lost control of smuggling rackets in Pelican Island, the amount of drugs in the prison has gone through the roof. I found an urgent letter from the Department of Prisons saying that drug-related deaths and overdoses on Pelican Island have gone up fivefold in the last two months. And it's all down to a drug the prisoners call frazzle.'

'Never heard of it,' Robin admitted.

'Frazzle is a form of cannabis, but instead of growing naturally from cannabis plants it's made in a lab,' Josie explained. 'It's twenty to a hundred times more potent than natural cannabis, and a pill the size of a peppercorn will get you high. It's popular in prisons because a thousand pills take up less room than a bar of soap.'

'Cut-Throat has to hear this,' Robin said, as he peeked out of the car and saw that Ollie was still in the enormous bread queue.

'While Alan worked prison staff, I looked into the drone defence system.'

'Did the translation of that Spanish document come back?'

'It was disappointing,' Josie said. 'It said the drone detection system had been sabotaged, but gave no clues on how they did it. Luckily the Super found a classified report from the Department of Corrections in Australia. The Aussies assessed twelve different drone defence systems and rejected the one used at Pelican Island, because . . . Hang on, I can't find the document.'

After a brief search, Josie began reading from the Australian report.

'*Real-world experience has shown that the CDS drone defence system can be rendered inoperable if the microphones are blocked by autumn leaves or bird droppings. Similarly, the system's microphones could be deliberately blocked by applying expanding foam or heavy tar-like paint. Preventing this type of sabotage would require regular visual inspections, which may not be possible where units are placed in remote or difficult-to-access locations.*'

'I could easily shoot those detectors with my bow and arrow,' Robin said. 'I bet I could hit them from thirty metres, even if the boat is bobbing around.'

Josie made an *mmm* sound.

'Why not?' Robin asked.

'If you shoot the drone detectors, the guards inside the prison will know because they'll stop sending signals,' Josie said. 'But if paint or bird droppings clog the microphones, they'll only know when someone takes a look.'

'Makes sense,' Robin agreed, 'but we'll have to get right up to the drone detectors. Some of the ones I spotted earlier were ten to fifteen metres up in the cliffs. And the guards might ignore kids spraying graffiti, but I bet they'll start shooting if they see us climbing prison walls.'

30. TRUE COLOURS

Cut-Throat drove a sporty Audi wagon to Lake Victoria, a journey of a few hours, compared to Diogo and Robin's full-day boat trip. An hour before the leader of Sherwood Brigands arrived, Ollie called and asked him to stop at a DIY store and buy a can of bitumen roof paint.

Diogo and Cut-Throat took *Dark Sky* straight out to Pelican Island for a detailed survey of the drone detection units. At the same time, Robin and Ollie walked to the boatyard behind their houseboat.

The yard was closed on a Sunday, but Ollie knew the owner and held spare keys. The pair experimented with brushes and foam mops taped to a variety of plastic oars and mast poles, trying to find the best technique for daubing a small amount of sticky black roof paint into the microphone at the centre of a parabolic dish.

Their eventual solution was a set of lightweight telescopic poles designed to paint the hulls of large boats, though Ollie swapped the huge brush for a washing-up sponge and fashioned a wire arm so it would easily reach inside the detector's dish.

Robin climbed a ladder to board a dry-docked yacht and hung a small piece of wood over the deck rail as a target, then they stood down by the keel and took turns using the pole to daub the target with paint.

This would be harder in the dark, so Ollie found a small torch and taped it near the top of the pole. Then they tried to see how far up they could reach, and realised they could get an extra couple of metres if Robin sat on Ollie's shoulders.

Dark Sky got back with the survey results just after they returned to the houseboat. While Ollie changed out of their paint-splattered dress, Cut-Throat sat at a table marking locations of detectors on a map of Pelican Island.

Cut-Throat had taken photos using a powerful zoom, and Robin clicked through them making notes on how difficult each detector would be to reach. Fortunately, King Corporation's cheapness had impacted the locations of the drone detectors.

'I swear they sent a couple of workers around with a long ladder,' Robin said, mostly to himself. 'Most detectors are less than ten metres above the water and located where there's shingle beach or low rocks.'

Robin was always happy when he was messing with computers or working out a plan, but the atmosphere became tense when Ollie came out of their bedroom, dressed in a dark grey tracksuit and holding a grubby denim jacket with their Brigands MC colours.

'I've been meaning to hand this back,' Ollie told Cut-Throat.

Cut-Throat turned away from his map and grunted.

'I've got no place in an organisation that won't accept me,' Ollie continued. Cut-Throat looked annoyed.

'I let you move up here and run drones when you started this Oliver/Olivia dress-wearing thing,' Cut-Throat said. 'Most of the lads said you'd shamed us. A lot of Brigands leaders would have dug a hole in the forest and buried you.'

'Nice of you not to kill me,' Ollie snapped back sarcastically.

The tension between Ollie and Cut-Throat made Robin think about the Brigands.

On the surface, their wild parties and anarchic lifestyle seemed cool. But the Brigands didn't admit women, they didn't tolerate trans or queer people and, now Robin thought about it, he couldn't remember a single non-white person at Insane Rob's party. Diogo's Mediterranean complexion was as diverse as they got . . .

If it wasn't for Marion, I'd tell Cut-Throat where to stick his drones.

And I'm never wearing Brigands colours again.

While Robin awkwardly considered the Brigands, Diogo tried to smooth things over by changing the subject.

'I have forest mushrooms and tomahawk steaks over on *Dark Sky*,' he said airily. 'Ollie bought beautiful French bread. We'll need a good feed before we head out to Pelican Island.'

31. MEN IN BLACK

It was a quarter to one in the morning as Robin checked himself in the mirror inside *Dark Sky*'s shower room. He wore black boots, dark grey jogging bottoms and a black hoodie with a black life vest over the top.

'Stop admiring yourself, I need to go,' Diogo said, as he thumped on the door.

Robin grabbed a backpack full of arrows and equipment and stepped through to the galley, where Cut-Throat and Ollie were dressed in black like Robin.

'Here,' Ollie said, gesturing for Robin to come over. Ollie picked up a tin of camouflage make-up from the kitchen worktop. 'I haven't used this since I was in the army. The smell takes me right back.'

Ollie daubed lines of the dark green make-up on Robin's forehead and cheeks and told him to rub it in. Robin saw how it looked reflected in the kitchen window and decided to take a selfie.

'Kids these days,' Cut-Throat said. 'Taking photos every two minutes . . .'

'How many followers have you got?' Ollie asked.

Since the tense scene earlier, Ollie and Cut-Throat had been getting along. But the way they kept agreeing and laughing at each other's jokes felt fake.

'I have zero followers,' Robin said. 'I'm a wanted criminal, so the government banned me from social media.'

'Time to roll, lads!' Diogo boomed cheerfully, as he flushed and exited the bathroom.

Dark Sky was too large and easily recognisable for an illegal operation, so the four black-clad figures jogged to the boatyard and launched two battered military-surplus rigid inflatable boats (RIBs).

Diogo and Cut-Throat rode in a large RIB with twin motors. It could seat six, and its forty-five-knot cruise speed made it an ideal getaway craft if things went bad. Robin and Ollie took a smaller single-engine boat. It was better for a stealthy approach to Pelican Island, but Robin had to squash in behind Ollie with his legs spread and the extendable poles hung over the back.

They rowed a hundred metres from shore before firing the noisy outboard motors. There was little moonlight and Ollie and Robin weren't expert sailors, so they took a tow from Diogo's RIB, which had the benefit of radar, GPS navigation and someone who knew what they were doing.

Apart from a few who worked night shifts, Pelican Island inmates were locked down with lights out by

9pm. The prison towers cut dark silhouettes in the sky, while the choppy lake blinked with yellow flashes from buoys marking the hundred-metre exclusion zone.

Cut-Throat had surveyed fourteen drone detectors, but when Robin looked at the map, he'd seen that taking out three detectors along the island's narrow eastern end would open a huge hole in defences and give easy access to the exercise yard where prisoners could meet drones.

Diogo released the line tethering the smaller boat as they neared the buoys. Lake Victoria was fed from the west by the Macondo and several smaller rivers. Water moving west to east was barely noticeable on the open lake, but Pelican Island deflected the flow and Ollie was surprised by the current as he attempted to row the hundred metres between the buoys and a sliver of shingle beach.

They'd hoped to approach in silence, but the current forced Robin to start the outboard motor. The flashing yellow buoy lights and graffitied sandstone cliff topped with twenty-metre walls felt ominous as they got close.

When the RIB neared the algae-covered rocks, Robin raised the motor out of the water, then hopped over the side and heaved the boat onto shingles.

Ollie grabbed the poles, and used graffiti markings to locate the spot directly beneath the drone detector. Robin jolted when he heard a clank at his feet, then realised he'd kicked a rusting can of spray paint.

Once the telescopic poles were extended, Robin ripped open a plastic bag containing a sponge soaked in the treacly bitumen paint. He hooked this to the end of the lightweight pole and clicked on the little torch.

Diogo's voice came from the radio attached to Robin's life vest, just as Ollie lifted the pole and squeezed the tar-soaked sponge in the centre of the dish to bung up the microphones.

'No boats on radar,' Diogo told Robin. 'How are you going?'

'So far so good.'

A three-minute cruise took the RIB to stop two, which was the most challenging. There was no graffiti here because thigh-deep water lapped against the cliff face. Ollie stood in the lake anchoring the boat, while Robin expertly climbed a three-metre boulder, slippery with spray and dark green algae.

Ollie passed the pole up, then Robin walked twenty metres along a narrow ledge, including a gap where he had to leap. The detector was three metres above Robin's head, so it was easy probing inside the dish and squelching the sponge.

'Prison transit on radar,' Diogo announced over the radio, and Robin heard retching as well as Diogo's voice. 'Keep low and hold position until it passes.'

'Copy that,' Robin said, as he squatted and turned to face the rocks. 'Are you OK?'

'Cut-Throat's a little seasick,' Diogo explained.

Robin crept along the ledge to a spot where a jutting rock gave cover, then peeked as the prison transit came around the island.

People joked that the boxy transit ferries that brought staff, inmates and prisoners to Pelican Island were older than the prison itself. It was an exaggeration, but the rust-streaked hulks were almost a century old, with coal-fired boilers that belched soot and a deck below where prisoners were chained to the floor.

But at two in the morning, the only passengers were guards, who smoked and chatted on deck as they headed home after their shift. Once they'd passed, Robin hurried back along the ledge, but was alarmed when he looked down and saw wash from the prison transit rising up to Ollie's neck and knocking them into the cliff. It took all their strength to stop the RIB breaking loose.

The third and final drone detector was on a broad stretch of beach with elaborate graffiti murals, including one urging people to vote for Robin's dad Ardagh in the upcoming sheriff elections.

Hundreds of spray cans littered the shingles, while beer bottles and disposable barbecues suggested that people didn't just sneak onto the island to snap selfies, but stuck around to party.

The detector here was the highest of the three. Robin thought he might have to piggyback Ollie to reach it, but the former biker found a ledge on a rock face and managed by themself.

'Decent night's work,' Robin said, glancing around and stifling a yawn as Ollie retracted the telescopic pole. 'I'm knackered, though.'

Ollie shivered. 'I'm soaked through. I need a bath and a brandy.'

Robin was about to radio Diogo and tell him they were ready to meet up and head home when a sharp crack made him jump. He shielded his face as chips splintered from the rock face, pelting his chest and leg.

Ollie was hissing in pain. When Robin turned, he saw blood coming from a wound on their cheek. A second blast hit further out into the beach and Robin realised a guard was shooting down from the prison wall.

'Shotgun pellets,' Ollie said, as a third blast rang out.

As Robin backed up to the rock face and shielded his face, he realised they were only getting hit by ricochets, while their boat had taken the main blast.

Robin gasped urgently into his radio. 'Diogo, they're shooting down from the prison wall. Our boat's full of holes.'

'Damn,' Diogo said. 'Maybe someone on that prison transit spotted you? Radar's showing a small boat coming your way at speed. I'm guessing they've sent river police to pick you up.'

'Can you get to us first?' Robin asked, as Ollie gripped his bloody neck.

'Probably,' Diogo said warily. 'But what's the point if that guard shoots my boat full of holes?'

32. WE'RE IN A TIGHT SPOT

Robin didn't know why he was different, but he felt it whenever there was danger. When others ran or got scared, Robin's brain got sharp and the world seemed to slow down.

The only light was yellow flashes from the buoys out in the lake, but it was enough for Robin to see Ollie's panic-stricken glances, and realise they were fussing over a couple of small cuts.

'Mate,' Robin said sympathetically. 'Take some breaths, you're OK.'

The RIB was on an open section of shingle beach with all of their gear inside. Robin feared getting shot if he moved away from the cliff face to fetch it, so he extended the telescopic pole and swung it towards his backpack in the rear of the boat.

He tried hooking his backpack using the wire on the end, but it was only designed to hold the paint sponge and it snapped.

'Balls!' Robin hissed.

For his second attempt, Robin threaded the end of the pole through his bow, which was strapped to the backpack.

Another shot blasted the shingles, though Robin now realised that at this distance shotgun pellets were more likely to be disabling than deadly. He used all his gym strength, but still strained as he raised the long pole with the bow hooked over the end.

He wasn't certain the bow was strapped tightly enough, but his backpack stayed the course as his bow zipped down the long pole, picking up enough speed to knock him back when it arrived.

If I don't get killed, I must tidy this bag.

Diogo's boat was supposed to be by the buoys less than two hundred metres from the island, but Robin saw no sign of it approaching. He pushed the button on his radio.

'Diogo, are you coming?' Robin asked, as he went down on one knee and unzipped his pack.

'Not looking good,' Diogo answered. 'There's now three guards on the wall. Two have rifles and they'll shoot us before we get near you.'

'Fantastic.' Robin sighed. 'And the police boat?'

'Two minutes away,' Diogo said. 'Can you creep across the beach and swim out to us?'

Robin groaned with frustration. 'I'm a rubbish swimmer, the current's strong, and I don't wanna get shot in the back.'

Robin poked Ollie, who was still in shock.

'I thought you were in the army,' Robin yelled impatiently.

'I hated the army,' Ollie shouted back. 'Turns out I don't like being shot at.'

Robin realised berating Ollie wasn't going to help.

'We have seconds till the river police get here,' Robin said, trying to sound encouraging as he grabbed Ollie's wrist to focus their attention. 'I need you to pick up as many spray paint cans as you can and throw them into our boat. Then stay close to the cliff face and shuffle along to shelter at the far end. OK?'

'I guess,' Ollie replied, after a painful pause. 'Where are you going?'

'Up,' Robin said, as he swung his bow over one shoulder and the stupidly heavy backpack over the other.

Ollie was startled as Robin leaped, found a tiny finger hold and began climbing the sheer sandstone cliff. The teenager's boots were designed for forest mud, not climbing, and at six metres up Robin lost a foothold and found himself dangling by fingertips.

At the same moment, the approaching police boat switched on a searchlight that blasted the cliff face with dazzling white light.

'You on the beach,' a speaker blared from the boat. 'Stand still. Put your hands in the air.'

The cops were looking for people on the beach, not six metres up the cliff face, but Robin felt sure he'd be spotted soon. Blinded by the searchlight and with the weight of his body, bow and backpack on three fingers, Robin reached sideways and felt for a second finger hold.

It felt like his shoulder was going to rip out of its socket, then he groaned with relief when he found a second hold to share the load. The ledge he'd been hoping to reach for was now less than half a metre above his head, but the foothold he could see was way out left and level with his waist.

'Keep your hands in the air,' the boat speaker repeated, for Ollie's benefit.

The police launch was as near to shore as its keel would allow. An armed officer vaulted over the side into knee-deep water.

Robin contorted his body to get his foot on the little ledge. With climbing shoes or bare feet, he could have curled his toes for extra grip, but all he could do was push his boot against the ledge and brace.

If his next move worked, he'd generate enough upwards momentum to grasp the ledge with both hands and pull himself up. Or he'd miss the ledge, fall seven metres onto the beach and wake up handcuffed to a hospital bed with a broken back . . .

33. FUN WITH EXPLOSIVES

The thick-soled boot gave no sense of grip. But Robin managed to grasp the ledge with his left hand. His right hand gripped too, but a jagged edge cut his palm as he pulled up his body and rolled onto the ledge.

Robin wiped blood on his tracksuit bottoms as he squatted on a ledge, forty centimetres deep and a couple of metres long. Overhead there was another few metres of cliff, and he hoped the jutting rocks made him invisible to the guards on top of the wall.

At beach level, two cops were now ashore, while a third stood on the rear deck of the little police boat. She had a rifle with a laser sight aimed at Ollie, who knelt at the far end of the beach, hands in the air.

Robin slid his backpack off and noted several rips from shotgun pellets as he began rummaging inside. There were snacks, schoolbooks, a random sock, weightlifting gloves, a shrivelled tangerine and several of Finn Maid's toy cars.

'Gotcha,' Robin said happily as his fingers felt the metal of a rectangular tin.

Inside were three arrowheads whose sharp tips had been filed away and replaced with tiny impact detonators and raspberry-sized blobs of plastic explosive.

A regular arrowhead dropped off the ledge and tumbled down the cliff face as Robin tugged it from its carbon-fibre shaft. After pushing on the explosive tip, he notched a regular arrow into his bow, then wiped more blood from his injured hand before slotting the explosive arrow and two regular arrows between his fingers for rapid reloading.

To Robin's relief, the cops below hadn't noticed the falling arrowhead, so he took a second to practise his aim. But he had to act before the cops coming up the beach got too near Ollie.

Robin's first shot was the trickiest. The cop with her laser-sighted rifle trained on Ollie was swaying with the boat. There was also a windscreen in the way. The cop's ballistic helmet ruled out a head shot and since police often wore stab-proof body armour, he couldn't risk shooting her torso either.

Robin watched a little wave lap over the boat then, as it dipped, he held his breath, took aim and shot a perfect arrow through the officer's thigh. The officer fired a shot as she collapsed, but the bullet hit the cliff metres above Ollie's head.

The second arrow had the explosive tip. Robin took

an easy shot towards the fuel tank at the back of their little RIB.

On its own the blob of explosive was enough to tear a door off its hinges or bring down a ceiling in an enclosed space. But the RIB's fuel tank added fire, and the graffiti paint cans that Robin told Ollie to throw into the boat made secondary blasts as they heated up and burst into spinning strips of metal.

'What was that?' Diogo shouted from Robin's radio. 'Are you OK?'

Robin didn't answer because he was fixing his aim on the other two cops. The first officer had caught the fireball and been knocked out. The second was limping towards the cliffs to take cover as Robin shot him in the arse.

'What's going on?' a prison officer shouted from the top of the wall, as smoke billowed up.

Robin had forgotten to zip his backpack after taking out the metal tin, and three arrows and a couple of school textbooks clattered down the cliff face as he hooked it back over his shoulder. After fixing the zip, he began a rapid downwards climb.

Robin notched an arrow as he hit the shingles. He checked that the cop he'd shot up the arse wasn't a threat. It hadn't penetrated far, but there was blood on the rocks where his head had hit the cliff and he'd knocked himself out.

'Diogo,' Robin said, pressing his transmit button as he ripped the cop's pistol from its holster. 'How many cops on a river boat? Could there be more than three?'

'Never more than three,' Diogo answered, to Robin's relief. 'There's still guards with guns on the wall, and the police searchlight doesn't help matters.'

Robin groaned before replying. 'I'll sort it out,' he told Diogo, then added, 'Since you're all basically useless . . .' to himself.

'Those cans!' Ollie said, still holding cuts on their bloody neck as they stumbled through the smoke towards Robin. 'I had no idea they blew up like that.'

'From primary school,' Robin explained as he glanced around, making sure the cop he'd shot in the water was still unconscious. 'Kid threw a deodorant can on a bonfire and blew his fingers off.'

'Is Diogo coming in to pick us up?'

'Too chicken,' Robin replied crossly, as he pointed at the police boat, which was starting to drift on the current. 'Think it's hard to pilot?'

'Throttle and rudder,' Ollie answered. 'A boat is a boat.'

'We must take the telescopic pole,' Robin ordered, keeping his bow ready as he began wading out to the police boat that was starting to catch the powerful current. 'If they find that, they'll know we're not graffiti artists. Now we need to ride this boat out of here, before the smoke clears and the guards up top realise we're getting away.'

34. ALL A BIT JAMES BOND

The burning RIB on the beach continued to spew dense smoke as Ollie threw the telescopic pole into the river police launch. As they climbed aboard, Robin was already on deck, stripping the semi-conscious officer he'd shot in the thigh.

After taking her gun, pepper spray, radio and helmet, Ollie helped to lift the officer up and dump her in the shallow water.

Robin put on the officer's ballistic helmet, then made sure she was stumbling towards dry land before opening the throttle and steering away from shore.

'Sorry I was a mess back there,' Ollie said. 'That whack in the neck made me freeze.'

'It happens,' Robin said. 'But it's good to have you back.'

Robin didn't want the guards on the prison wall to realise they'd hijacked the police boat, so he kept to a modest speed as he aimed towards the flashing buoys that marked the exclusion zone.

Diogo's voice came over the radio. 'Is that you in the police launch?'

'Both of us,' Robin confirmed, as he sped up slightly. 'Can you see the guards on the wall?'

'They know something went wrong,' Diogo said. 'But they're afraid to shoot into smoke and hit a cop. The bad news is, there's two more police boats heading our way. And you must kill that searchlight. It's giving your position away.'

Ollie started going over a switch panel, momentarily setting off a police siren before finding the switch to kill the light.

'What's my best direction?' Robin asked Diogo, as he glanced down at the police boat's radar. Diogo's RIB was a couple of hundred metres behind, while two police boats closed in from the south.

'South shore is nearest, but that's heading straight for the two police boats,' Diogo said. 'Aim towards the lights on the western shoreline. I'll try to draw at least one police boat off your tail.'

'Good luck with that,' Robin said, as he glanced behind and saw the flashing lights around Pelican Island receding.

Robin felt isolated as the little police launch skimmed the black lake. As he calculated that it would take twelve minutes to reach the lights on the west bank, he checked the radar and saw the two police boats about a kilometre behind.

While Robin drove, Ollie opened a metal trunk at the rear of the boat and found a bunch of police equipment, like cuffs, stun guns, flares and shields.

'The boats chasing must be the same because they're not closing,' Ollie said, as they stepped up behind Robin wearing a police helmet. 'But you can bet your life they'll have radioed ahead and have cops positioned along the shoreline.'

As Ollie said this, a half-metre-wide police drone shot across their bow. Then it circled and began tailing them, thirty metres above the water.

'Keep your voice low,' Robin warned, as he put the visor on his police helmet down. 'Those big drones have facial recognition cameras and microphones. Though hopefully boat noise will cover us.'

'Can you shoot it down?' Ollie asked, as spray drizzled down their helmet visor.

'Maybe,' Robin said. 'But I don't know what good it'll do us.'

'I've got an idea for getting away from cops when we reach dry land,' Ollie said. 'Have you got any arrows that go bang?'

'Two,' Robin said.

'There's a waterfront marina here,' Ollie explained, as they tapped a spot on the navigation screen. 'It's where wealthy folks moor yachts and cruisers. At the northern end of the marina are two big fuel tanks. They're situated away from the boats for safety.'

'What's your plan?' Robin asked.

'Suicide run,' Ollie said. 'We'll aim towards the fuel tanks at full speed. You fire one of your exploding arrows and blow the tanks sky high. At the last second, we dive off the boat and escape underwater as everything gets blasted to hell.'

'Sounds a bit James Bond,' Robin noted. 'And I'm not a fish. How am I supposed to breathe underwater?'

Ollie pointed to the metal trunk. 'We have two sets of gear for police search divers. Have you ever been diving?'

'I'm not even keen on swimming,' Robin admitted. 'Is it complicated?'

'How long until we reach the west bank?'

'Six minutes,' Robin guessed. 'Maybe seven.'

'I did a two-week diving course in the army,' Ollie said. 'So I might have to skip over some details.'

Ollie saw Robin's worried look. 'You saved me on the beach, now it's my turn,' he told Robin firmly. 'I'll fit your air tank and breather and we'll jump together.'

'What about my bow and backpack? All my homework's in there.'

Ollie smiled. 'Tell teacher your homework exploded in a fireball when you jumped out of a stolen police boat.'

Despite the tense situation, Robin managed to smirk. 'I already used that excuse.'

'You need to lose that drone, or they'll know what we're up to,' Ollie said.

Ollie took the controls as Robin grabbed his bow. The speeding boat gave a reasonable aiming platform and the big drone made an easy target. Except it dodged the incoming arrow.

'Cops have upgraded,' Robin moaned indignantly. 'Damned thing has collision detection.'

Robin saw that he only had four more arrows in his bag as he pulled two out. He shot them in quick succession, the first making the drone dodge left, into the path of a second arrow that tore it apart.

'Nice shooting!' Ollie shouted, as the drone spiralled down.

The drone shot up briefly as it was flicked by the wake from the speeding boat, then landed dead in the water.

'You're too buoyant to dive,' Ollie said. 'Lose your boots, trousers and life preserver.'

As Robin quickly stripped to shorts and T-shirt, Ollie kept one eye on the boat while setting up Robin's oxygen tank and breathing mask.

'What about wetsuits?' Robin asked, as Ollie held up the tank for Robin to fit his arms through.

'No time to put them on,' Ollie answered, as they buckled straps around Robin's waist and chest, then checked that the breathing mask was working. 'Are you shaking?'

'Water's the one thing that gives me jitters,' Robin admitted.

'As long as you can still shoot straight enough to hit a ten-metre-high fuel tank,' Ollie said, thumping Robin on the back, 'you're gonna be fine.'

35. COLD, WET AND BARELY DRESSED

As the villas and restaurants along Lake Victoria's western embankment got closer, Ollie steered left and noted that one of the two police boats had broken the chase.

While Robin sat at the back of the boat fitting his last two arrows with explosive charges, there was chatter over the boat's police radio. The signal kept breaking up, but the gist was that there were several police cars distributed along the western shore and three drones patrolling the sky.

'Why so much manpower for graffiti kids?' one officer asked.

'Suspects are believed to be Robin Hood and one unidentified companion,' the police controller answered. 'Detectives on Pelican Island found carbon core arrows and schoolbooks with Robin's name.'

Another cop cackled jubilantly. 'Promotions all around if we catch that little prick.'

As Robin fitted his last explosive arrowhead, Ollie jumped back from the steering column and yelled, 'Where the heck did that come from?'

'What?' Robin asked, as he saw a large boat closing in on the radar screen.

'It appeared on radar from nowhere and it's right behind us.'

Robin had experienced something similar on Diogo's smuggling boat in the Eastern Delta.

'Must be a prowler,' Robin said, suddenly sick with nerves. 'They're jet-powered boats that use stealth tech. You don't see them on radar until they're practically on top of you.'

'Customs and Immigration have prowlers,' Ollie said. 'Not cops.'

Robin didn't get time to answer before the enemy came into view.

'That's a prowler,' Robin yelled. 'We're *so* screwed.'

The boat had the same basic design as the prowlers Robin had encountered in the Delta, but this one was dark blue instead of matt black and had a higher superstructure more suited to police work.

'Stop your engines or you will be fired upon,' the police prowler's loudspeaker blazed, as it neared them. It was eight times the size of the river police launch and its jet engines sounded like a vacuum cleaner from hell.

A bank of six massive searchlights on the front of the prowler lit up. Robin notched his explosive arrow, but the dazzling light made it impossible to aim.

'Stop your engines,' the loudspeaker repeated. 'We are authorised to use deadly force to capture terrorists.'

As the prowler drew closer, the wash thrown up by its bow began flooding the back of the launch.

'I've lost rudder,' Ollie yelled desperately.

As Robin felt water above his ankles, he glanced behind and saw that they were still hundreds of metres from shore. Feeling that the wash from the prowler was about to knock him off his feet, Robin blindly let his explosive arrow loose.

Two of the prowler's six searchlights shattered, but the explosion licked harmlessly off the boat's angled superstructure and didn't even crack a window.

'We're sinking,' Ollie warned as the engine cut out. 'We have to—'

Before Ollie could say 'jump', there was another explosion, far larger than a blob of explosive in the tip of an arrow could produce. A massive fireball erupted from the prowler's rear deck. The ship's nose shot into the air and the inlets to its twin waterjets made an ear-splitting whine as they left the water.

'That wasn't my arrow,' Robin gasped.

'We have to jump,' Ollie said, as they pulled up Robin's breathing mask and turned on his oxygen. 'Lock your arms around my waist and whatever you do, *don't* let go.'

'What about your air tank?'

'It's not ready.'

The prowler was about to smash back in the water and make a wave that would suck their boat under the larger vessel. 'Grab me now! Now!'

The instant Ollie felt Robin's arms around their waist, they leaped into the water. Robin was shocked by the blackness and brutal cold under the lake, but Ollie kicked powerfully, holding his breath for twenty-five metres.

Robin was terrified and sobbed when Ollie kicked up to the surface to breathe. In the background the prowler seemed stricken, with no engine noise and listing to one side like she was flooding.

'Ready?' Ollie gasped, then dived back underwater with Robin clamped on.

They swam further this time. When Robin came up to the surface the prowler's searchlights were barely above the water, while cops in life vests swam towards an inflatable yellow raft.

'Tread water while I catch my breath,' Ollie said.

Robin wasn't sure how to take his breather off, so he just nodded.

'Don't be scared,' Ollie said as he let Robin go. 'We'll make it to shore.'

As Ollie took some breaths, they learned that Diogo had sensibly invested in waterproof radios.

'Guys, are you out there?' Diogo's voice crackled desperately. 'Tell me you didn't get sucked under.'

Robin left his radio when he stripped off, but Ollie still had a unit clipped to their tracksuit top.

'I'm a hundred metres west of a sinking prowler,' Ollie told the radio. 'I'm not as fit as I used to be, but we'll make it to shore.'

'We're near,' Diogo said. 'We tried to get to that prowler sooner, but . . .'

A narrow beam of light caught Robin's damp cheek.

'Cut-Throat sees you!' Diogo said, almost tearful. 'On our way.'

The black military RIB was designed not to be seen in darkness, but its engine buzzing across the lake was the sweetest sound Robin had ever heard. Cut-Throat looked like a man who'd spent two hours being seasick, but still used one monstrous, tattooed arm to fish Robin out.

'Kid's good with an arrow, but he's no water baby,' Ollie joked, as they flopped down in the back of the RIB, gasping for air.

'We tracked you on radar right up until you sank,' Diogo said, as he glanced around suspiciously, then gunned the RIB's powerful engines. 'We even fished Robin's bow out of the water.'

Robin sat up enough to see it and smiled. The string would need replacing, but his pricy bow looked OK.

'What happened to the prowler?' Robin asked, shivering as he used Diogo's canteen to wash the taste of lake water from his mouth, then tore open a foil emergency blanket.

'As you left Pelican Island, I noticed speckles on the radar screen,' Diogo explained. 'They moved too fast to be anything other than a stealth boat, so I tracked it as it tried to intercept you.'

'How'd you blow that beast up?' Robin asked, as he shivered under the blanket.

'It's been tough for smugglers in the Delta since Customs and Immigration brought in the prowlers. But we've discovered a weakness in the prowler's fuel tank. While the cops in the prowler had their attention focused on you, I crept up behind, hiding this RIB in the prowler's wake, where radar doesn't work well.

'Cut-Throat managed to stop puking for a couple of minutes and I steered close enough for him to fling a few of sticks of demolition explosive onto the prowler's rear deck. When that goes bang, the shockwave cracks a prowler's fuel tank. And the engines run on high-octane fuel, so the first tiny spark inside an electrical switch and the whole ship goes bang.'

'Genius,' Robin said, as the wind blasting through the speeding boat tried to tear off his foil blanket. 'So, where now?'

'Cops are all along the west bank,' Diogo said. 'We need to get off the water before a drone spots us, so we'll blast a few kilometres south. Find an inlet where we can abandon this boat. Then it's a ten-k hike back to Ollie's place.'

'On a cold night, in my underwear, with no boots,' Robin moaned.

'Things could have turned out worse,' Diogo noted. 'And maybe Cut-Throat will give you a piggyback.'

36. MONDAY MORNING MISERY

Danielle changed cell assignments so that two of Marion's Super Seven pals got moved out and replaced by wannabe Mafia 13 member Guppy and a girl with thick glasses who everyone called Bottle Head.

Marion's cousin Freya was still the toughest girl in the cell, and she moved Marion to the bunk below hers for protection. Guppy got the silent treatment from her new cellmates and she got Marion's old bunk, overlooking the stinking squat toilet.

Pelican Island's meat processing facility was a seven-day-a-week operation, so Marion worked a full shift on Sunday. At 6am Monday, a nineteen-year-old guard who inmates ironically nicknamed Grandma clanged her stun stick between cell bars to wake Marion up.

'Rise and shine, Miss Maid! Another fine day is upon us.'

Marion's legs ached so bad that she almost fell as she got out of bed. Her cellmates yawned and swore as she stumbled barefoot between tightly packed bunks.

'Sarika's back from hospital today,' a girl yelled from another cell as Marion passed. 'She'll mess you up good.'

Marion found enough energy to flip the girl off. The girl bared her teeth and hissed like a snake.

'Don't I get breakfast?' Marion asked, as they passed the dining area. 'Or a drink at least?'

Grandma tutted as she unlocked the first exit gate. 'Inmates who attack guards get diddly squat.'

'Nobody's impressed, you know,' Marion told Grandma. The control room buzzed the second exit gate and they stepped out into the yard outside Stable Block. The sun was rising.

'What are you cackling about, inmate?' Grandma sighed.

'Acting tough and copying older guards like Danielle,' Marion said, as gravel dug into her bare feet. 'Did you ever consider acting like a human being?'

Grandma chuckled as she slammed the outer gate. 'Maybe I became a prison guard because I was a little girl who pulled heads off dollies and threw bricks at the neighbour's cat. Now shut your pie slot and move.'

It was a twelve-minute walk through Central, across a second courtyard and into the frozen meat warehouse.

Marion felt wretched when she saw the changing bench near the entrance, with her oversized boots, insulated gloves and overalls frozen stiff with yesterday's sweat.

The work was monotonous and Marion fought boredom by creating lists in her head: *Ten favourite video games, ten hottest actors, first five things I'll do when I get off Pelican Island.* She was less than two hours into the shift and pushing a trolley stacked with boxes of chipped beef when the warehouse's PA system called out: 'Inmate 8471, Maid.'

Grandma stood at the entrance, displeased that she'd been made to walk across the prison a second time.

'Lose your work gear.' Grandma sighed, then threw brand-new prison-issue shoes at Marion's feet. 'Wear those.'

'What's happening?' Marion asked as she peeled her thick gloves.

Marion expected no answer, but Grandma shrugged and spoke gently. 'Been thinking about what you said on the way over, Maid. I guess this prison would be better if we all lived in harmony.'

'Cool,' Marion said, smiling but not convinced.

As Marion unzipped her insulated suit, Grandma jabbed her in the belly with her stun stick. It was only the low power setting, but still enough to double Marion over.

'Then again, zapping inmates is *super* fun!' Grandma said, as Marion scowled and clutched her stomach.

The new shoes made Marion wonder if she was being escorted to the prison admin block to be questioned about the washroom riot. But Grandma led her through meat processing to the locker room where she'd change before her old job working the giant food mixers.

A little mound of stuff had been set out on a changing bench in front of Marion's old locker. There was a new toothbrush and toothpaste, plus a comb, a thick towel and set of prison uniform unlike any Marion had seen before: deep colours, no rips or cigarette burns, and new socks and underwear with cardboard tags.

'Wash and change,' Grandma ordered. 'You've got ten minutes.'

Marion wondered if she'd got her old mixing job back, but that didn't explain the new clothes. She tried to ignore Grandma staring as she took her first shower in three days. It was satisfying drying on a towel that didn't feel like sandpaper and pulling the cardboard tab from underwear without stains from the hundreds of inmates who'd worn it before.

Marion grew anxious as Grandma led her from meat processing to Central, then into a section of the prison with carpets and *Staff Only* signs everywhere. With no other inmates and no sign of CCTV, Marion imagined a secret room where the SWAT officer she'd zapped would be waiting with a stun stick and several burly colleagues.

She was right about the small room, but the only person inside was a nurse. He told Marion to lie on an examination bed then looked at her feet, which had been chewed up by walking barefoot and the heavy men's boots in the warehouse.

'Bit of a mess,' the nurse said cheerfully. 'Nothing time and care won't fix.'

Marion remained on edge as the nurse sprayed disinfectant on her feet and fixed a plaster over a cut on her left heel. The nurse gave Marion extra socks and a paper bag containing four painkillers, padded dressings for her heel and a little tub of antiseptic cream.

'Come on, princess,' Grandma said, as she checked the time on her phone. 'Back to Stable Block.'

It was five to nine when Marion got back to her cell block. The dining area seated thirty, so meals were served in three shifts. As Marion arrived, second shift was clearing breakfast trays, while the thirty girls on third shift queued along the cell block's narrow hallway.

'Make space for the inmate,' Grandma ordered.

Marion drew stares as she crossed the dining area with damp combed hair, new shoes, new uniform and the little paper bag of dressings and medicine. She realised she was being put on show as she shuffled past the queue, close enough to say 'Hey' to Freya and get tuts and hisses from Mafia 13.

Danielle sat in the control room and Grandma gave her a wave to open the door of Stable Block's observation cell. This single cell had two CCTV cameras and a toughened glass window instead of bars.

All new arrivals on Pelican Island spent their first night in an observation cell. Usually observation just had a bed, sink and toilet, but an office chair and a small table had been brought in. As Grandma ordered Marion inside, the inmates saw a well-stacked breakfast tray, plus a cream donut and a can of iced coffee.

'Thanks for your help, inmate,' Grandma announced, making sure everyone in the hallway heard as she crashed the metal door shut. 'Danielle will be in to take your statement shortly.'

Marion was tempted by the donut, but as she turned back, she saw the young women heading to and from breakfast. Her friend and fellow Super Seven member Lola peered in the window, looking confused, while Guppy gave Marion a two-fingered salute and kicked the door.

'Grassing won't save you,' Guppy shouted. 'We'll get to you. Even in protective custody.'

As Ice Lolly spat on the outside of the window and made a throat-slitting gesture, Marion hurried up to the glass and shouted after Lola, but the queue had moved on towards the dining room.

'Lola, I swear I've not grassed,' Marion shouted desperately. 'They're making it look like I'm a snitch, but I'm not.'

Marion wasn't sure how much Lola heard over all the noise, while girls coming out of breakfast saw Marion's new uniform, combed hair and fancy breakfast.

'Snitches get stitches,' one girl screamed, as fists pounded the door and spit streaked down the window.

Marion hoped Freya and the rest of the Super Seven trusted her enough to see through the ruse. But the rumours that shot around Stable Block often bore little relation to the truth. It would be tough convincing her friends that she hadn't snitched, and she'd have zero chance with Mafia 13 girls who already hated her guts.

37. FARTS OF DOOM

It was just after ten when Ollie hopped from their houseboat onto *Dark Sky*, which was moored alongside.

'Anyone up?' Ollie asked, as they opened the sliding door into the galley.

Robin was awake, messing with his phone as he lay on a narrow mattress on the galley floor.

'Thought there'd be more room in a boat like this,' Ollie noted.

Robin looked up from his phone and sighed. 'Have you ever shared a room with Cut-Throat? First, he smokes a cigar before bed. Then he takes his boots off, and I swear that guy hasn't changed his socks in a year. Cut-Throat's farts count as a chemical weapon and when he finally sleeps, he snores so loud that my bed shakes.'

Ollie laughed. 'If you're sticking around, you're welcome to sleep on my houseboat.'

'I'll take that offer,' Robin said enthusiastically. 'Floor's hard and this mattress is trash.'

'Did you see our escapade made the news?'

Robin nodded. 'I saw an article about the chase and the prowler sinking. And the river police released pictures of my history textbook and science project.'

'Your penmanship really needs work,' Ollie joked, as one of Cut-Throat's bigger snores tore through the boat. 'Crikey, that *is* loud!'

'Imagine trying to sleep in the same room.'

'Interesting thing is, I've seen no mention of us destroying drone detectors,' Ollie said.

Robin got off the floor and winced in pain.

'You OK?'

Robin showed Ollie a sole covered in scuffs and grazes. 'That's two hours walking over nettles, reeds and cow pies.'

'If the news is right, the cops think our plan was to lure them out and sink their new prowler.'

Robin laughed noisily as he grabbed a carton of orange from the fridge. 'Channel Fourteen says the police prowler cost seven million. River police only took delivery last week.'

'Nobody seems to realise we were there to sabotage drone detectors,' Ollie said. 'But there's only one way to be sure.'

'Put up a drone and see if we can fly over Pelican Island,' Robin said, between gulps from the carton. 'We'll have to be careful. There'll be untold cops looking for us.'

'Mostly you,' Ollie pointed out. 'But I know this part of the lakefront better than anyone. There's only one road and a million hiding places.'

Cut-Throat kept snoring as Robin breakfasted on bread and leftover steak. He put on jeans and socks, then went to the master bedroom and told Diogo he was going out.

Over on the houseboat, Ollie had fitted an Ishtar T7 with a fresh battery and made an eight-hundred-gram care package that included chocolate, razor blades, whisky and two packs of cigarettes.

'I won't risk sending a phone until we know the detectors are down,' Ollie said, as Robin watched them attach the package to the drone's belly with two rubber bands.

Robin kept low in the back of Ollie's ancient Renault for the five-minute drive out to the pontoon. After deciding that Robin would fly the first run, Ollie told him to wait until quarter past ten, when there would be bikers in the prison exercise yard.

With the weekend over there was hardly any traffic on the lake, and the water-skimming flight to Pelican Island's eastern tip was uneventful. As the drone closed on the graffiti-strewn cliffs, Ollie watched it on a tablet, while Robin flew with first-person-view goggles.

The speeding drone gave them a brief glimpse of the beach where they'd battled the night before. Their RIB had burned so hot the sand beneath had turned to glass. There were also chunks knocked out of the sandstone cliff where the spray cans exploded.

The beach seemed deserted, but just in case, Robin flew to the second disabled detector, where he'd climbed the rocks. His nerves peaked as he tilted the drone back for the climb up the prison wall. As it reached the top, it clipped a curl of barbed wire and spun out of control.

'No!' Robin gasped, as **ERROR** and **OVERRIDE** flashed up in his goggles. He thought the T7 would smash into the rocks, but the drone's emergency stabilisation took control and brought it back to a stable hover above the rocks.

'I didn't see,' Robin explained. 'It came up so fast.'

'Battery is down to fifty-two per cent,' Ollie noted.

'Do I abort?'

'The drone is half the weight on the way home, so it uses less battery. You should be OK, but there's no margin for error.'

Robin flew the drone back to the top of the wall, taking care to avoid the wire.

'Controls are tilting left,' Robin said. 'Maybe the package shifted when I hit the wire.'

'Damaged propeller, more likely,' Ollie said, as they watched the screen. 'Nothing you can do about it except stay calm.'

The T7 didn't cut out as it passed over the wall, but Robin found the vista across the prison a bewildering jumble of towers, factory roofs and exercise yards.

'Cut right and climb towards the yard on the eighth floor of Central,' Ollie explained. 'The tenth floor has the helipad – it's the roof below that.'

Robin skimmed over a flat factory roof and an abandoned courtyard with the gallows where prisoners used to be hanged. He swept the drone up the side of Central tower past tiny cell windows. Then he crossed a fence into a puddled prison-exercise yard with soccer pitches, basketball courts and lots of guys drifting around in prison-issue shorts and hoodies.

'Bikers control the weight pile,' Ollie said. 'It's on your right, past the guy in a wheelchair.'

Robin saw guards in a tower overlooking the yard as he cut right. As promised, the rusty barbells, dumbbells and chin-up bars were surrounded by large, bearded men. Robin made a perfect landing between two weight benches and the bikers knew what to do.

Robin's view turned to a pink blur as a biker picked up the drone and freed the package.

'Forty-three per cent battery,' Robin noted anxiously. 'Is that enough to get back?'

'We'll find out,' Ollie said. 'I fitted the bigger props and isolated motors to keep the noise down, but I guess they use more battery.'

Once the package was off, the biker set the drone down on top of a weight bench, and it took off and flew over the smiling bikers.

'We're back in business!' Ollie said as they did a happy jump.

The drone felt fast and responsive without the cargo attached, but the return flight took longer because Robin kept speed down to maximise battery life. While Robin flew, Ollie prepared another T7, with a package containing two tiny phones plus chargers and spare batteries.

'Three per cent remaining,' Robin gasped as he landed the drone and dashed onto the pontoon before the wind caught it. 'Too close for comfort.'

The drone felt hot after the long flight. It was splattered with dead bugs and one propeller was mangled from the barbed wire.

'I'll pilot this next one,' Ollie said, as they took the FPV goggles and linked them to the other drone. 'Once we get phones across, we can coordinate landings and make sure we're sending what guys on the inside want.'

'Sounds good,' Robin said cheerfully, as he leaned against Ollie's rusty Renault and watched the second drone shoot towards the island.

38. THE MINISTRY OF CULTURE

Cut-Throat liked people to believe he was deranged and uncaring, but leading a bike gang for twenty years without going to jail or getting murdered takes brains and cunning.

Robin cracked up when he got back to *Dark Sky* and saw Cut-Throat squashed at the little galley table. He looked studious, with reading glasses halfway down his nose, laptop open and surrounded by scribbled notes.

'You laughing at me?' Cut-Throat growled, in a way scary enough to wipe the smile off Robin's face.

Robin changed the subject. 'Drones are working. We dropped two phones on the second run and Ollie's gonna recharge batteries then head out to do a third.'

'He texted me already,' Cut-Throat said dismissively, then looked up and smiled. 'You did the job. I owe you one.'

Robin opened the fridge. He was pleased to see that Diogo had been to the supermarket as he picked out Rage Cola and a pork pie.

'If it's OK, I'll stick around for a couple of days and make sure everything keeps working,' Robin said. 'Ollie lost most of their drones, so they've ordered three of the new Ishtar T8s. I can help them hack the software, and we've ordered custom motors and props that are super quiet.'

'Grab us a beer while you're over there,' Cut-Throat said. 'Cops will be looking for you on the river and major roads. Sticking here until things settle down makes sense, but there's other houseboats and a lot of workers in the boatyard, so keep your head down.'

Robin nodded as he crossed to the table and handed Cut-Throat his beer. He saw that the Brigand leader was looking for financial statements, and each scrawled note was about one guard who worked on Pelican Island.

'Your girlfriend sent more stuff through,' Cut-Throat explained, as he popped his beer.

'Ex-girlfriend,' Robin corrected.

Cut-Throat laughed. 'With all those fans, you'll soon have more girls than you can handle.'

Robin didn't want a conversation with Cut-Throat about his love life. 'Can I help you find something?'

'The staff on Pelican Island are almost as crooked as the inmates,' Cut-Throat said, as he tapped one of his notes. 'But I spoke to a biker on the inside while you were out. I'm sure this guy, Jay Patel, is bringing in the frazzle flooding the prison.'

'They listen to prisoners' landline calls,' Robin said warily, as he sat across the table from Cut-Throat.

'I know what I'm doing, kid,' Cut-Throat said, as he pushed his reading glasses up his nose. 'I've been dealing with prisons since before you were born.'

'Josie mentioned Jay Patel,' Robin said. 'His godmother, Anne Kemp, is deputy warden and she got him a cushy three-day-a-week job as an Arts and Crafts teacher.'

Cut-Throat nodded. 'Patel earns more than most guards who work full-time, but you should see what he spends his money on.'

Robin found it excruciating watching Cut-Throat stabbing laptop keys with one fat finger as he tried to use the computer. Finally, he clicked on a link to Jay Patel's TwoTu shopping history.

'Lego!' Robin said, smiling as Cut-Throat scrolled down a list of hundreds of Lego sets, along with the price Jay Patel had paid for them. 'He's spending thousands! He must buy every set they bring out.'

Cut-Throat nodded. 'The guy I spoke to this morning says there are approximately thirty inmates in the Arts and Crafts programme. It's not paid for by the prison service, it's funded through a special grant from the Ministry of Culture's Outsider Art programme.'

'What's outsider art?' Robin asked.

'I just looked that up,' Cut-Throat said. 'Most art is done by posh types who went to art school. Outsider art is made by people who are mentally disabled, unemployed or prisoners. My mate doesn't know how inmates get picked for Arts and Crafts, but reckons they come from every wing of the prison. Men, women, juveniles. Even the geriatric unit.'

'Any bikers in Arts and Crafts?' Robin asked.

Cut-Throat shook his head as Robin paused to think.

'Sounds like a great system for smuggling drugs and other gear through the prison,' Robin said. 'You've got an art teacher who can bring in paint, clay and other messy stuff that guards won't want to search. You've got inmates from every part of the prison to distribute the drugs, and the scheme is masterminded by the deputy warden who's supposed to stop drugs getting in.'

'And she installed detectors to stop Ollie's drones,' Cut-Throat said bitterly.

Robin stared at the papers spread across the table. 'We could send this information to the cops.'

Cut-Throat stared at Robin like he was an idiot. 'Cops are hopeless. Brigands solve our own problems.'

'What then?' Robin asked.

'First step is to pay Jay Patel a little visit,' Cut-Throat said, with a slight air of menace. 'You can ride along if you like.'

39. FIRST LIE BECOMES TRUTH

After Stable Block's third breakfast shift, its ninety inmates walked to prison factories, or the outdoor courtyard for recreation time.

Danielle let Marion stew in the observation cell for a few hours and seemed pleased by the spit and chewed-up food that inmates had daubed on the window when she finally came to unlock.

'Stand when a guard enters, inmate,' Danielle snapped as she entered the cell. 'I see you enjoyed your food.'

Marion got off the bed, rubbing tired eyes. 'Freya and my friends won't fall for your trick,' she said as she stifled a yawn. 'They know I wouldn't grass.'

Danielle cracked her nasty smile. 'Inmate, there's an old saying that goes *The first lie becomes the truth.*

'Some inmates will figure out that I set you up to look like a snitch. But in a few days, what everyone will remember is that you disappeared for a few hours. When you came back, you had new clothes, you got special food and your punishment duty in the warehouse was over.'

Marion couldn't hide a smile. 'I don't have to go back to the warehouse?'

'Back to mixing,' Danielle said. 'Someone made a fuss about you working with male prisoners, so now I'll have to find another way to make you miserable.'

Marion hoped she wasn't being tricked again. 'I'm not the only person who ever hit a guard,' she said bitterly. 'Why have you got it in for me?'

'Discipline,' Danielle said. 'When the other girls look at you, they see what happens if they piss me off.'

Danielle called Grandma on her radio. The teenaged guard didn't appreciate having to walk to meat processing for a third time, and her expression could have curdled milk.

Marion didn't let herself believe she'd got off punishment duty until she was back in her hooded overall and white rubber boots. Kerry the supervisor looked pleased when Marion walked onto the production floor.

'Running a mixer isn't brain surgery,' Kerry said. 'But you'd be amazed how few inmates can follow a list of ingredients on a touchscreen.'

Marion smiled. 'Did you complain about me working in the warehouse?'

Kerry didn't admit it, but did say, 'Danielle is not my favourite person.'

A week earlier, Marion couldn't have imagined wanting to go back to the steamy heat of the mixing room, but stepping up to the gantry above the two huge mixing bowls felt like a triumph.

The pace of the mixing job varied and Marion spent the first part of the afternoon standing idle while the room next door packed batches of minced beef that had no additives. She used the time to rebuild her little den, with a chair made from fifty-kilo salt bags.

Her first mixing job was an eye-watering recipe for samosa filling. It contained curry powder, chilli flakes, four sacks of dehydrated potato cubes and a chemical called eugenyl methyl ether, which tasted like ginger but was cheaper than the real thing.

'You're back!' Marion's mate Paul yelled, as he opened the metal chute from the plant's upper level.

'How's life?' Marion asked.

'My youngest visited yesterday,' Paul said. 'Taller than me now. He's a fan of your mate Robin, and was chuffed when I told him I'd met you.'

'I'll sell you an autograph for twenty quid,' Marion joked.

Mixing felt easy after the ruthless pace in the warehouse, but Marion still felt queasy as the package of raw minced beef, blood and fat slid down the chute into the huge bowl. To make matters worse, the samosa mix was bulked out with minced chicken liver that gave off a metallic urine smell.

As Marion grabbed a giant metal paddle and used it to scrape clumps of meat stuck in the chute, she noticed a shadowy figure moving behind Paul. For a second she thought he was going to shove Paul down, but the guy dropped a thick butcher's glove onto the chute.

'What the . . . ?' Marion gasped, as the glove landed on top of the gory mixture and the top of the chute clanked shut.

Marion always ignored the cockroaches, chunks of plastic packaging, sticky labels and the odd frozen mouse that appeared in her mixing bowl. But butchers' gloves are reinforced with metal wires to prevent fingers getting lopped off, and Kerry wouldn't be impressed if it clogged the outlet pipe.

'Dickhead,' Marion moaned to herself as she used the paddle to draw the glove to the edge of the mixing bowl, then pulled on a disposable glove and stretched over the guard rail to fish it out.

The glove was gross, spattered with blood and liver, but as Marion crossed the gantry to dump it in the trash, she realised the fingers were rigid, like something was pushed down inside.

After a wary glance at the ceiling-mounted cameras, Marion started the mixer paddles with her clean hand, then retreated into her den between racks and gave the glove a shake. A clean, viciously sharp butcher's knife dropped out onto a shelf.

Knives were tightly controlled in the factory, and possession would earn you a week in a punishment cell. But on the other hand, it was a useful last resort if she got attacked again.

The contents stuffed in the other fingers were fatter. Squeezing the tip of the longest finger made a King Crunch chocolate bar drop out. This had always been Marion's favourite, and it made her certain that the glove was a gift from biker friends.

Then she squeezed the last rigid finger and beamed as a tiny phone and charging plug hit the metal shelf.

'Holy guacamole!' she spluttered, as she cast a wary glance to make sure nobody was nearby.

Marion beamed as she pressed the *on* button. The phone was the size of a man's thumb with a tiny amber-on-black display screen.

She flipped through a list of stored numbers – Dad, Indio, Karma, Lucy, Matt, Robin. There was also a text from Robin, telling her to set a PIN so nobody else could use the phone.

Apart from Aunt Lucy, everyone on the list was a wanted criminal. None of them could visit Marion without getting busted and she wasn't even allowed to speak to them on the prison's landline phones.

Marion glanced over at the giant mixer's touchscreen panel and saw there were still two and a half minutes on the countdown timer. The phone had ninety-six per cent battery and one signal bar, and Marion had no doubt who she wanted to speak to first.

'Hello,' Marion's birth mum Karma answered, sounding suspicious because she didn't recognise the number.

'Hey, Mum!' Marion sniffled, as tears welled in her eyes. 'It's me!'

40. MEAN, MOODY AND MENACING

One of the worst things about being Robin Hood was having to hide in the trunk when he rode in a car. And of all the trunks Robin had sampled, Cut-Throat's Audi wagon was the nastiest, with sharp knives and axes, a carpet soaked in engine oil, a pair of stinking biker boots and stains left by Cut-Throat's Rottweilers that Robin preferred not to think about.

He sweated under a dog blanket while Cut-Throat stopped at a shopping park to buy clothes and a Lego set. When Cut-Throat finally opened the wagon's rear door to let Robin out, they were in a deserted garage block behind a housing estate, twelve kilometres south of Lake Victoria.

While Cut-Throat swapped forest boots and Brigands colours for loafers and grey cardigan, Robin put on a new pair of unbranded canvas skateboard shoes and a Minecraft T-shirt. Since Robin was small and nothing about his face was particularly distinctive, he'd pass for the biker's pre-teen son, if you didn't look too hard.

'Take this,' Cut-Throat said, handing Robin a carrier bag with a large Lego set inside, then taking an axe from the car's trunk and hooking it through his belt. Robin left his bow because it was a huge clue to his true identity.

The estate's terraced houses looked decent, though vandalised delivery scooters and a graffiti-strewn playground suggested a rough neighbourhood.

Number 38 had a new Ford charging on the driveway. The woman who answered the door in a green sari seemed surprised by Cut-Throat's bulk, while Robin was surprised by Cut-Throat's attempt to sound civilised.

'Good afternoon,' Cut-Throat said. 'I'm here to see your son about the Lego sets he advertised.'

'Step in, take off your shoes,' the woman said, backing away from the door, then shouting up the stairs. 'Sanjay, your guest is here.'

The woman regretted asking Cut-Throat to take off his shoes, as his crusty sock aroma filled her hallway. Fortunately, Jay Patel was hurrying down garishly carpeted stairs while pulling a *Star Wars* T-shirt over his hairy belly.

'Lego's in the shed,' Jay said.

As Jay led Robin and Cut-Throat through the kitchen and to a shed that took up half the garden, Robin realised that Jay's greasy hair, Yoda slippers and tracksuit bottoms were exactly how he'd imagined a thirty-two-year-old who lived with his mum and spent all his money on Lego.

'Wow!' Robin said, genuinely impressed as Jay pulled a big sliding door and exposed a shed with Lego spaceships dangling from the ceiling, a huge Lego train set along the back wall and shelves lined with hundreds of unbuilt Lego sets.

Jay was keen to show his collection. As well as turning on the main light, he lit three glass display cabinets, and flicked a switch to start a Lego passenger train.

'Expensive hobby,' Cut-Throat said as he admired a bright yellow castle. 'I built that when I was a kid.'

'Set 375,' Jay said proudly. 'It's very hard to find with the stickers in mint condition.'

Cut-Throat stepped closer to Jay and stopped using his polite voice. 'I was wondering how a guy who earns three thousand pounds a month can spend four thousand a month buying toys from TwoTu.'

Jay's eyes opened wide. 'I don't think my finances are your business,' he mumbled. 'The sets you came to buy are on the chair, and I see your boy has the ski resort we agreed to swap.'

Cut-Throat ignored what Jay was saying. 'I guess a godmother who's deputy warden makes it easy to smuggle drugs.'

'I think you're talking nonsense,' Jay said, backing up to his Lego trains and looking like he was about to faint.

Cut-Throat plucked a large blue spaceship from the ceiling and smashed it against the floor.

'Come on, man!' Jay gasped.

'Could I jog your memory?' Cut-Throat said, as he looked over at Robin.

Robin reached into the carrier bag and handed Cut-Throat printouts of Jay's bank statements and online purchases.

'You're a naughty boy,' Cut-Throat said. 'Someone set you up an overseas savings account with over fifty thousand pounds. Your mum has a new car on the driveway. Admit it. You smuggle drugs to Pelican Island.'

'Please,' Jay pleaded. 'I have no idea what you're talking about.'

Cut-Throat broke the wings off a biplane, then leaned towards the train set.

'Not my trains,' Jay begged.

'Former staff don't have it easy when they get sent to prison,' Cut-Throat warned. 'Ten years minimum for smuggling drugs. And I have biker pals who can make your stretch exceptionally unpleasant.'

Jay looked like he was about to cry. 'It's not my set-up,' he blurted. 'I was unemployed for two years and my godmother Anne offered me a job. A guy comes here with a bag of stuff. I take it across on the prison transport and hand it to an inmate in my class. I'm just a courier. I never look inside.'

Cut-Throat looked intrigued. 'Nobody searches the stuff?'

'The X-ray hasn't worked since I got the job,' Jay said, as his hands trembled. 'The guards do manual searches, but they just peek inside.'

Cut-Throat growled. 'Jay, the question is: do I take my information to the drug squad at the nearest police station, or will you help me out?'

'Help how?' Jay said, as he stared at his Yoda slippers.

'When the next bag of stuff for the prison arrives, you call me so I can inspect the contents. I'll also need you to let a couple of my pals into Arts and Crafts class.'

Jay wiped sweat off his brow and nodded. 'The bag's no problem. Adding people to the class is harder. They just send people.'

'Figure something out,' Cut-Throat said firmly.

'OK,' Jay said, as Cut-Throat pointed at Robin. 'Do you know who this guy is?'

Jay had been too intimidated by the giant biker to pay Robin any attention.

Cut-Throat gave a clue. 'He usually carries a bow.'

'Robin?' Jay said, squinting in disbelief. 'But he's so tiny.'

'Hey!' Robin spat, then furiously punched in the front of a Lego fire station.

'Kid's touchy about his height,' Cut-Throat explained. 'But he's hacked you good. We'll be tracking your phone's GPS, your calls, social media and messages.

And since I don't trust technology, I'll have some of my boys keeping you under surveillance too.

'Don't think about telling anyone about this meeting, *especially* your godmother. Unless you want to spend the next decade behind bars with my biker pals using your head as a toilet brush.'

'OK,' Jay agreed, as he rubbed a tear from one eye.

'You tell me when that bag arrives,' Cut-Throat ordered, then stood on a Lego brick as he turned to leave the shed. 'OWWWWWW!'

41. CHARGING PROBLEMS

Two days after Cut-Throat confronted Jay Patel, Robin stood at a workbench aboard Ollie's houseboat using a magnifier and a tiny screwdriver to fit quiet motors to three newly arrived T8 drones.

He was giving the first batch of four motors a test run when his phone rang.

'Hey, mate,' Marion said affectionately. 'Have you saved the world yet?'

'Working on it,' Robin answered, enjoying Marion's voice for the first time in months. 'Everything OK?'

'Prison's *so* fabulous,' Marion said. 'Except the senior guard who likes to torment me and the gang that wants me dead.'

'I thought you might call sooner,' Robin said, sounding a little sore.

'The battery on this tiny phone doesn't last,' Marion explained. 'Charging is a nightmare.'

'Aren't there sockets in your cell?' Robin asked.

'Sure, Robin,' Marion snorted. 'But to use them I'd have to unplug the big-screen TV or the massage chair.'

'How was I supposed to know?' Robin said defensively.

'There are wall sockets in meat processing where I work,' Marion explained. 'I'd like to take the phone back to my cell so Freya can use it, but cells get searched all the time and there's at least one girl in my cell who'd snitch if she saw it.'

'So, you're at work now?' Robin asked.

'My supervisor is on lunch and I have two minutes and eighteen seconds while my machine mixes a thousand kilos of Norwegian meatball paste.'

'What's the difference between Norwegian meatballs and Italian meatballs?' Robin asked.

Marion laughed as loudly as she dared. 'We haven't spoken in months. We have two minutes to talk and that's your question?'

Robin found something more important to discuss. 'I still feel bad about you getting caught. I should have made sure you were in the other car when we left that bus station.'

'Everyone makes mistakes,' Marion said. 'I guess mine was taking part in that stupid robbery.'

'Karma's looking after your share of the money,' Robin said.

'Fat lot of good it does me in here,' Marion said.

'I'm setting up drones that can carry more stuff,' Robin said. 'So let me know if there's anything you need.'

'Poison for Danielle the guard,' Marion said, only half-joking. 'Slower-acting, so she suffers before she croaks.'

Robin laughed. 'I could use something like that for Alan.'

'I forgot that!' Marion snorted. 'Matt told me Josie dumped your ass.'

'You don't *sound* very sorry,' Robin noted.

'You kept Josie longer than I expected, considering you're totally self-centred and immature.'

'Me, immature?' Robin protested, then realised Marion was winding him up. 'I had more fun when you were around.'

'I'll be back in ten to twelve years,' Marion said. 'If I don't get stabbed first.'

'Maybe I'll take out a few guards with my bow and bust you out,' Robin said.

'I wish,' Marion said, as her mood drooped. 'Josie said she was looking into escape plans, but it's been eighty years since an inmate got off Pelican Island.'

'Wait,' Robin said irritably. 'You spoke to Josie before me?'

'Indio got everyone at Sherwood Castle together,' Marion explained. 'All the Scarlocks, Unai, Azeem. Even Mr Khan said hello.'

Robin laughed. 'Did Khan ask why you hadn't done any homework for six months?'

'I wouldn't put it past him,' Marion said, then made a little gasp. 'Mixer's making a weird noise. Gotta go!'

'Speak again soon,' Robin said hopefully, but Marion was gone.

42. A COOL FIVE MILLION

Robin had finished installing the custom motors and was reattaching the bodyshell to a T8 drone when Cut-Throat and Diogo came aboard carrying two large pizza boxes.

'Dig in,' Diogo urged, putting the boxes on the table as Robin hurriedly moved a bunch of screws and little drone parts. 'One meat monster and a pepperoni.'

'Ollie's out meeting their miniature phone supplier,' Robin explained, as he grabbed a slice of meat monster. 'Where'd you guys disappear to?'

Cut-Throat explained as he held up a canvas shopping bag. 'Jay Patel called. His delivery guy dropped off the stuff he's supposed to smuggle into Pelican Island.'

'What was it?' Robin asked.

'Phones, dental floss, batteries and this,' Cut-Throat said, as he pulled a clear plastic cylinder from a bag. Inside were several thousand tiny white pills.

'Frazzle?' Robin asked.

Cut-Throat nodded as he handed the cylinder over for Robin to inspect. 'A thousand pills from a dodgy laboratory cost five hundred quid. On Pelican Island they're ten pounds each.'

'I haven't counted,' Diogo said, 'but there's three to five thousand pills in that cylinder. If Jay Patel brings in three cylinders a week, that's at least a hundred thousand weekly profit.'

'Five million a year,' Robin calculated, then whistled as he passed the little cylinder back to Cut-Throat. 'So, what are you gonna do with all those pills?'

'If Jay arrives at the prison with no pills, they'll know we're on to them,' Cut-Throat explained. 'So, we'll switch the pills for fakes.'

'You'll have to find pills that look exactly the same,' Robin pointed out, as he took another slice of pizza.

'Labs make frazzle look like those zero-calorie sweetener tablets so they're easy to smuggle,' Diogo explained. 'I can buy pills that look the same for a few pounds in any pharmacy.'

'And when inmates find out they spent ten quid on a sweetener?' Robin asked.

'That's when the fun starts!' Cut-Throat said, then broke into a booming laugh. 'I wouldn't want to be a Mafia 13 pill pusher after selling fake pills to a bunch of violent criminals.'

Robin was amused by the thought, but Cut-Throat hadn't finished.

'When the dust clears, I can use drones to send in the real frazzle and the bikers will be back in their rightful place: bossing the other gangs and making bundles of cash running every racket on Pelican Island.'

'Wait!' Robin gasped. 'You're not going to stop the prison getting flooded with drugs? You're taking the business over?'

'Well, duh!' Cut-Throat said.

Robin dropped his pizza and spluttered. 'I helped get the drones running so you could get phones and snacks to Marion. You didn't tell me I was helping you to set up a five-million-a-year drug-smuggling operation.'

'Calm down, kid,' Cut-Throat said. 'You've done a great job and you'll get your cut. Two per cent of my gross for the first year. It'll be at least a hundred thousand pounds. All I ask in return is that you sort things out if there's more problems getting drones in.'

'I don't want drug money,' Robin said furiously, as he remembered the warning Karma gave when he left Sherwood Castle: *Cut-Throat can turn on the charm when he needs something, but never forget he's the ruthless leader of a motorbike gang.*

'More cash for me then,' Cut-Throat said with a shrug.

Robin felt his face burn with anger. If Cut-Throat wasn't Marion's dad, he might have grabbed an arrow and shot him.

'I'm one of the good guys,' Robin spat.

Cut-Throat snorted as he rammed pizza in his mouth. 'You break laws all the time.'

'But I'm trying to make the world better. I'll happily break the law to call out Gisborne's corruption or steal stuff that Forest People need. But the only thing that improves when you get prisoners hooked on frazzle is your bank balance.'

'Every prison has drugs,' Cut-Throat said. 'If we don't sell 'em, some other gang will.'

Robin looked down at the T8 drones on the table. 'Ollie can finish fixing these. I want nothing to do with this.'

Diogo followed Robin as he stormed off the houseboat and hopped across to *Dark Sky*.

'I'm an idiot,' Robin told Diogo furiously. 'Karma warned me that Cut-Throat was dangerous. Once I got the drones working, why wouldn't someone like him use them to move drugs?'

Diogo put a hand on Robin's shoulder. 'You *have* helped Marion, which is what you came here to do. And Cut-Throat isn't completely wrong; there are drugs in every prison.'

Robin tutted. 'But in other prisons I'm not responsible for how they get smuggled in.'

'I try to be a good person, and so do you,' Diogo said, as he pulled Robin into a hug. 'But if you spend your life trying to make the world perfect, you're gonna go crazy.'

43. LANDING IN CLOVER

'Danielle is messing with our heads again,' Freya Tuck said, as the muscular sixteen-year-old sat with her legs hanging off a triple bunk.

After breakfast, inmates either went to work or out to the exercise yard. But it was now quarter to ten and Freya, Lola, Sophie and Marion remained in their cell.

'Maybe they forgot us,' Lola said, as she lay on her middle bunk.

Marion shook her head as she peered through cell bars and into the empty hallway. 'We're all Super Seven. It's too much of a coincidence.'

'This is Danielle,' Freya repeated, tipping her head back and staring at the ceiling graffiti.

'Is she on duty today?' Sophie asked.

Marion groaned. 'Danielle's always on duty. I swear she does overtime because she enjoys tormenting me.'

'She's mean because she never gets home to sleep,' Lola speculated.

'You only have to sleep if you're human,' Sophie pointed out.

As the girls laughed, a barred gate clanked at the end of Stable Block's central hallway. Marion peered out and saw the elderly guard Ruth limping down the hallway on her bad hip.

'Laverne, McTavish, Maid and Tuck,' Ruth said grumpily as she opened the cell door. 'Get your shoes on, I haven't got all day.'

'Where we going, boss?' Lola asked, as Freya jumped off her bunk.

'Education block,' Ruth said, as Sophie led the four friends out of the cell.

'For actual education?' Lola said sarcastically. 'Not mincing dead cows, or sewing designer dresses?'

Ruth tutted. 'Don't give me a hard time, girls. I don't run this joint.'

'How's your hip today?' Freya asked as they reached the exit at the end of Stable Block's main hallway.

'Arthritis,' Ruth said, then spoke into the intercom next to the exit. 'Taking four prisoners out, open the outer gate, please.'

Ruth waited a few seconds and was about to try the intercom again, when Danielle stormed from the control room, stopping by Ruth with hands on hips.

'Why aren't these four at work already?' Danielle steamed. 'Did you forget them?'

Ruth scowled at her boss. 'Could you read the roster before shouting at me?'

This enraged Danielle, especially when Lola sarcastically parroted, 'Yeah, Danielle, read the roster!'

'Shut your hole, inmate,' Danielle growled, then looked at Ruth. 'What does the roster say?'

'Education block, Arts and Crafts.'

Arts and Crafts was the cushiest assignment on the island. But while the three girls smiled, Marion worried about the phone she had stashed in meat processing.

'I haven't authorised anyone to transfer to Arts and Crafts,' Danielle said, then scowled at Marion. 'Certainly not *this* one.'

Marion was tempted to poke her tongue at Danielle, but satisfied herself listening to Ruth's explanation. 'Paperwork came from the deputy warden's office. Shall I wait while you call to check?'

Danielle blew out her cheeks. 'Take 'em,' she grunted.

Ruth rolled her eyes and gave her boss a mocking salute. 'Aye, captain!'

Danielle looked like her head was about to explode as the four girls laughed.

The education block was a short walk, just past Stable Block's exercise yard. Marion was surprised to find herself inside a modern two-storey building. If you ignored the barred windows, it could have been some posh private school. The classrooms all had padded chairs, smart whiteboards and laptops, but zero pupils because King Corporation had fired all the teachers.

The exception was the Arts and Crafts space. The plaque on the door said **Proudly funded by the Ministry of Culture**. After a little hallway where a guard sat reading a book about fighter jets, they entered a workshop, bigger than three regular classrooms.

There were tables for drawing, pottery wheels and woodwork benches. Skylights filled the room with morning sun, while large, barred windows gave an impressive view over the lake.

'Seems you girls landed on your feet,' Ruth said.

There were about thirty inmates spread over the workshop. Most sat around chatting, though a couple were actually making art, including an elderly inmate carving a huge fist from a tree stump.

Lola's eyes were drawn to four juvenile boys. 'Dibs on the hottie with blue eyes and floppy hair,' she said.

Sophie nodded. 'As long as I get the brunet with biceps.'

'Boys!' Freya said, shuddering. 'So gross.'

'Hope Mr Biceps fares better than Sophie's last boyfriend,' Marion joked.

Sophie laughed. 'I only brutally murdered one boyfriend. You don't have to keep going on about it . . .'

The girls had set each other off laughing, and everyone stared as Ruth led them to a desk with a floppy-haired man behind it.

'Sanjay Patel?' Ruth asked.

Jay nodded as he stood up and signed a handover sheet. He eyed the girls suspiciously, especially Marion.

'It's free and easy here,' Jay told them. 'Toilets up back. Use any equipment you like, but sharp things are locked up and you can only take one at a time. We all get along – no fighting or showing off. If there's trouble, you'll be sent back to whatever job you had before.'

Freya looked confused. 'Do you teach anything?' she asked, as Lola headed off to talk to the boys.

'Try and make something,' Jay said. 'I have to send photos to the Ministry of Culture, and there's supposed to be an exhibition next year.'

The girls saw distinct groups as they looked around. One set of male inmates sat at the far end playing cards while elderly men had their spot by the windows. Adult women colonised the large art tables, and juvenile boys sat atop woodwork benches, swinging their legs.

Freya smiled as she led Marion to a spot next to some shelves, with floor cushions and a rack of inspirational art books.

'This is incredible,' Freya whispered to Marion as she flipped through a book on Picasso. 'Yesterday I was in the laundry looking at skid marks.'

'Those two are boy-crazy,' Marion said, as she pointed at Lola and Sophie chatting by the woodwork benches.

'I bet this is something to do with your dad,' Freya said. 'He got the phone to you. Now the bikers have found a way to change work assignments.'

'I'm worried about my phone,' Marion said. 'It's in the mixing room.'

'Well hidden?'

Marion nodded. 'Way up on a high shelf, behind tubs of celery powder.'

'If an inmate finds it, they'll just steal it,' Freya said.

Marion nodded. 'I set a PIN, so nobody can use the phone, but it's covered in my fingerprints. If a guard finds it, I'm done for.'

44. BURN IT DOWN!

Marion worried less about the phone after one of the lads told her that Arts and Crafts was only three days a week. She'd be back in the mixing room tomorrow, and perhaps she'd figure a way to smuggle the phone across to Arts and Crafts, where Freya, Sophie and Lola would be able to share it.

It was energising being around boys for the first time in ages, though Marion wasn't as excited as Lola and Sophie. A sixteen-year-old called Trent kept making bad jokes and flirting with Marion. But when Freya told Trent who Marion's dad was, he looked terrified and bolted to the other side of the workshop.

The lads all wanted to know stuff about Robin Hood, so Marion told them some stories. They were all gripped when Freya described how she and Marion first met Robin by a forest stream, unconscious and bleeding from a head wound.

'Your hero would have been bear food if I hadn't piggybacked his ass through the forest,' Freya said dryly. 'And he bled all over my good orange hoodie.'

This got a big laugh, then a fourteen-year-old called Bukayo looked at Marion. 'But if Freya hadn't rescued Robin Hood, you wouldn't be in prison.'

This thought spoiled Marion's mood, but it still felt like the best day in ages. Then class ended and the quartet walked back to Stable Block. Danielle had finished her shift; dinner was a disgusting vegan pie and there was the usual pre-lockdown face-off with Mafia 13 in the bathroom.

But nothing seemed out of the ordinary until forty minutes after lights out. First, everyone who was dozing off got woken by a siren in the juvenile male cell block a few hundred metres away.

As everyone lay awake, a row kicked off in Marion's cell between Guppy and her bunkmate Jade, who'd just arrived from another prison.

'That pill you sold me was trash,' Jade whispered, kicking the bottom of Guppy's mattress.

'Don't touch me,' Guppy spat back.

'Give me my tenner back.'

Guppy laughed. 'It takes a while to kick in, dummy.'

'I've taken frazzle before,' Jade said.

'Idiots, shut up!' Freya boomed. 'Or I'll be down to knock your heads together.'

Guppy and Jade both did what they were told and Marion felt content, knowing one of the toughest girls in Stable Block had her back.

But as Marion drifted back to sleep, shouts started going back and forth between cells.

'This ain't no frazzle!'

'Yeah!' someone else agreed. 'Fake-ass drugs.'

'There be trouble if I don't get my money back!' another inmate warned.

As one row turned physical in a cell down by the dining room, Jade got off her bunk and punched Guppy in the face.

'I want my ten back, now!' Jade shouted.

'I got friends,' Guppy warned as she tried to punch back. 'I'm Mafia 13.'

'Ain't got no tattoo.' Jade laughed. 'You're barely a hanger-on.'

As Marion put her pillow over her head, there were shouts in all ten cells and fighting in three.

'Do not make me get out of bed,' Freya warned, as Jade yanked Guppy off her bunk.

The new arrival underestimated Guppy's strength and found herself pinned to the cell floor getting punched.

The other recently arrived inmate in Marion's cell, Bottle Head, was friendly with Jade, so she jumped off her bunk and began twisting Guppy's foot.

As Freya jumped down to sort them out, Lola yelled anxiously, 'Stop it! If SWAT comes, we'll get the snot beaten out of us.'

The thought of a SWAT team filled Marion with dread. Freya pulled Guppy off Jade and flung her towards the nasty hole-in-the-floor toilet.

Marion slept with her feet by the cell bars, but now she swapped around to peer through the bars and down the hallway. Stable Block was often noisy, but Marion had never seen fights in multiple cells at the same time, and they all seemed to be sparked by a dodgy batch of frazzle.

Marion's stomach tightened as the emergency alarm went up. She knew a SWAT team was coming, and if it was the same crew as last time, they'd smash her.

45. ROOFTOP BAD BOYS

The alarm made Marion's ears ring. There was enough light to see a girl across the hall get her face slammed against the bars by two Mafia 13 girls. Further down, there was smoke and a flash of orange.

Moments later, a screaming girl frantically tried to kick a burning bedsheet under cell bars and into the hall.

'Fire!' Marion gasped, looking around as Freya returned, triumphantly grinding a fist into her palm.

'If we stay calm, the SWAT team might wear themselves out dealing with the other cells,' Freya suggested as the smoke hit her nose.

Sophie, Lola and the others all looked through the bars as more smoke filled the hallway and girls in the cell opposite totally lost it, throwing stuff, slashing mattresses and beating the hell out of each other.

'SWAT should be here by now,' Sophie said.

At the far end of the hallway, a pregnant guard called Amani threw a bucket of water over the burning sheet, but the smoke coming out of that cell was getting out of control and girls had their faces against the bars, trying to breathe.

'Open the cell!' Marion shouted desperately, though she couldn't be heard over the alarm.

'Where's the SWAT team?' Freya asked, now almost wanting them to arrive to calm things down. 'They're never more than a couple of minutes.'

'Busy?' Marion suggested. 'We heard the other alarm.'

At the far end of the hallway by the dining area, Amani and a senior guard called Stuart looked clueless. The smoke coming out of the cell with the fire inside was getting super thick and, as Marion looked up, she noticed smoke curling through a light fitting.

'If they don't let us out, we'll fry,' Freya said, as Marion felt the smoke start to burn her eyes.

The SWAT alarm cut off, but a quieter smoke alarm kept bleeping and now you could hear girls shrieking and begging to be let out of the burning cell.

As Amani ran from the washroom and threw another bucket of water at the flaming bedding, her colleague Stuart realised inmates would die if he didn't evacuate the cells.

Ten cell doors clanked open, and Stable Block's ninety inmates began surging into the smoke-filled hallway.

'Stay back!' Stuart ordered as he unlocked the inner gate, then ran to the control room and pressed the button for the outer door.

Amani was knocked flying as girls charged from the cells. Some even enjoyed stepping on the pregnant guard's hands and kicking chunks of a burning pillow at her as they escaped.

Marion's cell was at the far end of the hallway. The smoke was still getting thicker, but Lola had turned on the tap above the grotty cell toilet and was using it to soak T-shirts and washcloths.

'Put these over your face,' Lola shouted. 'And keep low.'

Guppy snatched a ragged wet towel and tied it over her mouth as she ran for the exit. Marion and Freya were the last girls out of the last cell. Escaping the choking smoke, they leaped over burning bedding and slivers of melting mattress covers that drifted on currents of hot air.

Marion was desperate for breath by the time she reached the thickest smoke, outside a cell whose three triple bunks were rectangles of orange flame. She hurdled a flaming pillow and a melted shoe but, as she landed, a hand grasped her ankle.

Marion knew she'd choke if she opened her mouth, so she frantically tugged the back of Freya's shirt. The smoke was too thick for Freya to see the woman on the floor, but she understood when Marion started dragging a body.

Freya found something to grab amidst the smoke and helped Marion pull. As they neared the exit, Marion realised they were dragging Amani the guard. Both girls moaned when they took a breath of clean outdoor air, then stumbled and fell to the gravel.

Stuart had grabbed a shotgun before locking up the control room. He had the panicked air of a man who knew he was alone with ninety crazed inmates.

'Everyone away from the building!' the guard shouted as he waved the gun. But his tone changed when he saw that Marion and Freya had saved his pregnant colleague.

'She's breathed a tonne of smoke,' Freya told the guard, as Marion glanced around the chaotic exercise yard. 'She needs water.'

There was no way anyone could get over the barbed-wire-topped fence around the exercise yard, but reality wasn't stopping some hysterical inmates from trying. Guppy had been knocked out in one of the many fights, while coughs spewed from another group of girls in a rowdy queue for the yard's two drinking fountains.

As Marion gobbed out a mouthful of sooty spit and wiped herself down with the wet towel she'd used to cover her face, she looked beyond the fence and understood why the SWAT team hadn't showed.

Two dozen teenaged inmates had found their way to the roof of the boys' unit. Now they were tearing up concrete tiles and using them to pelt the SWAT team trying to smash through a barricade and enter the building.

It was hard to see what was going on further off in Central and the women's prison, but to Marion there seemed to be smoke and alarms all over the island.

'Whole prison going berserk,' Marion told Freya, before erupting in more coughs. 'It doesn't take much to tip this place over the edge.'

46. SMOKE ON THE WATER

The sun rose over the lake as Robin awoke on a bunk inside Ollie's houseboat. He immediately sensed something was wrong: Channel Fourteen news blared from Ollie's laptop in the dining area and the correspondent was talking about Pelican Island.

When Robin peeled back the curtain over the porthole beside his bunk, he saw neighbours standing on their houseboats, staring across the lake.

A military helicopter thudded overhead as Robin yanked on jogging bottoms. He hopped over to *Dark Sky* barefoot and found Ollie and Diogo on deck. Smoke wafted from the west side of Pelican Island, while the sky above buzzed with news drones, police choppers and a big double-rotor army helicopter landing on top of Central.

'What did I miss?' Robin gasped.

'See for yourself,' Diogo said, as he passed Robin his binoculars.

Smoke made it hard to get a clear view, but as Robin scanned across the island, he saw shirtless prisoners streaking along the outer wall, bedsheets with scrawled slogans hanging from cell windows, and a guard tower with a burnt roof and every window smashed.

'Have we heard from Marion?' Robin asked anxiously.

'Not directly,' Diogo said. 'Local news said there was a fire in her block, but everyone evacuated safely.'

As Diogo said this, a TV inside *Dark Sky* said, 'Two hundred and fifty troops were flown in to restore order after rioting broke out in three separate locations. So far there have been no reports of fatalities, but fire has gutted the prison's central kitchen and four injured prison officers have been flown to nearby hospitals . . .'

'We knew the fake pills would cause trouble,' Ollie said. 'But not like this.'

Robin shook his head. 'One package of fake frazzle *can't* have caused all this.'

'Apparently it did,' Ollie said. 'Cut-Throat has spoken to bikers on the inside. Trouble kicked off everywhere when inmates realised their pills were junk. It was more than SWAT teams could cope with.'

'Pelican Island's warden has said that over ninety-seven per cent of the prison is back under control,' the TV continued. *'But adult male prisoners remain in control of some areas of the ten-storey building known as Central, while a group of young male offenders are holding a protest on the roof of their housing block.'*

Cut-Throat came out of the galley, dressed in his filthy jeans with all his chest tattoos on display.

'I spoke to more of our guys, and it's fantastic,' Cut-Throat said cheerfully. 'Mafia 13 are getting pummelled by everyone who got sold a dodgy pill. Bikers are taking control of Central.'

'Great,' Ollie said, though Robin and Diogo didn't share their enthusiasm.

'We must keep our supply lines running while Mafia 13 is crippled,' Cut-Throat said. 'Most inmates are locked down in their cells, but I've got one inmate doing emergency maintenance who can collect pills we drop in the exercise yard. I want our people supplying frazzle as soon as the emergency ends and prisoners can leave their cells.'

Ollie looked at Robin. 'I'll need to make three or four drone runs this morning,' they began. 'The customised T8s are amazing, but with so much air traffic, I could use a good pilot.'

Flying drones into a prison while helicopters buzzed and things were on fire sounded like mad fun, but Robin shook his head.

'Maybe drugs always get in prisons,' Robin said. 'But I want nothing to do with it.'

Diogo saw the scowl on Cut-Throat's face and spoke quickly to ease the tension. 'The cops are going to have their hands full dealing with the prison riot,' he said. 'I think I'll take *Dark Sky* back east. I can drop Robin near Sherwood Castle.'

'Sounds good,' Robin said, but he felt sad that things would end awkwardly with Ollie and Cut-Throat.

'You're turning down a lot of money,' Cut-Throat warned Robin. 'There's six thousand inmates on Pelican Island and at least half do frazzle to take the edge off.'

Robin wanted to tell Cut-Throat that he was a slimeball, but the teenager didn't want to add the volatile gang leader to his long list of enemies.

'I don't want to stop overnight on the most dangerous part of the river,' Diogo told Robin. 'I'll cast off before dark and cruise through the night. That should get us to Darley Dale Dam by tomorrow lunchtime, and you home the morning after.'

47. HURTY GRAVEL BITS

The dense smoke had been terrifying, but Stable Block's bare walls and spartan furnishings were designed to stop fires started by inmates from taking hold. A two-person fire crew dealt swiftly with burning mattresses and clothes, then gave the pregnant guard Amani oxygen as they waited for a helicopter to take her to hospital.

Smoke and water damage meant the girls couldn't return to their cells. As morning broke in the exercise yard, Marion and eighty-nine fellow inmates were in severe pain. After getting rounded up by soldiers, they'd spent the night kneeling in front of the yard's wire fence, with hands on their heads and gravel digging into bare knees.

Defiant shouts and roof tiles still came down from the boys' prison, but the girls had orders to stay still.

'I have to pee,' one girl begged, as she stumbled to her feet and turned around.

Before the inmate took a step, a soldier in full body armour bounced her against the fence, then whacked an extendable metal baton across her stomach. As the girl crashed to the gravel, a SWAT team officer wrenched her arm behind her back, then forced her back to her knees.

'Eyes front!' another soldier screamed at Marion, as she realised she'd unconsciously turned her head towards the action.

'Anyone else want the toilet?' the SWAT officer shouted sarcastically. 'Maybe you'll think about this pain before trashing your cells again.'

After another hour frozen still, with knee and shoulder pain and a smoky itch in her throat, Marion glimpsed her floor supervisor Kerry entering the courtyard with a soldier on either side.

Kerry discussed something with a SWAT officer, then started randomly pulling inmates out of the line, more than fifty prisoners away from Marion. An excruciating stab of pain in Marion's back made her brave enough to shout.

'Kerry, can I come?'

'Shut your mouth, inmate!' a soldier blasted terrifyingly.

Marion heard boots behind and braced for a kick, but Kerry had recognised her voice.

'Marion,' Kerry said as she rushed over, then looked at a SWAT officer. 'That one's a good worker. I'll take her for sure.'

'All right, missy. On your feet,' a soldier shouted.

Marion stumbled as she stood up. Her shoulders ached, the back of one leg was numb after being in the same position for hours, but the most pain was from her knees, which were full of dents where the gravel had dug in.

Marion hobbled to the edge of the yard. She hadn't found her shoes when she'd escaped the smoke-filled cell block, so she faced another barefoot walk to the meat processing plant, with added danger from shattered roof tiles and broken glass.

Kerry and the two soldiers marched Marion and nine other girls through passageways and courtyards that crackled with shouts and tension. Soldiers with machine guns stood by every gate, looking scary. In several spots they passed groups of male inmates who'd been captured and left stranded on their bellies with feet and ankles hog-tied behind their backs.

'Listen up,' Kerry said, after leading the ten girls into the changing area that Marion used when she worked the mixers. 'I'll give you time to use the toilets and drink some water. Then put on boots and gloves and head upstairs. We lost power to refrigeration during last night's troubles, so all animal products have got to be dumped.'

'What about breakfast?' someone asked.

'Only if you want raw meat,' Kerry said, then after a pause, 'The prison kitchens are out of action, but I'll do my best to source you girls some food.'

Girls who'd never worked in meat processing were grossed out as they climbed spiral stairs to the first floor and saw the huge refrigerated rooms full of meat, offal, blood and fat. Marion had only ever glimpsed the upper level through the chute, and though she was hungry and tired, she located the spot above her mixer and imagined Paul working there.

'Inmate, less wandering, more lifting!' a white-coated supervisor shouted.

Marion grabbed one of the wire trolleys that butchers used to move stuff around and walked into a cold room where girls had begun dragging out giant slabs of beef. Filled trolleys had to be wheeled through giant folding doors to the plant's outdoor loading dock, then down a ramp to a stinking trash barge.

The work was similar to Marion's punishment duty in the warehouse, but the pace far easier and the girls had a few macabre laughs. One inmate found a bag of sheep's eyes and they got thrown around until Kerry told them to knock it off.

Another girl squealed when a bag of cow's blood burst open, while a slight girl slipped as she tried to tip two hundred kilos of ground beef into the barge. She wound up thigh-deep in minced beef and trash bags, then almost got shot by a soldier on the dock who thought she was trying to escape.

While Kerry escorted the tearful girl from the trash barge to the showers, Marion decided to take a breather by sneaking into a little side room where all the butchers' knives were chained up inside a wire cage.

She assumed the space was empty, but was startled by a beanpole biker with a maintenance cart and grubby yellow overall.

'Cut-Throat's daughter, right?' the guy said, all wavy arms and twitches.

'Sure.' Marion nodded, turning away because the guy's breath was vile.

'Boss asked me to pass on a message if I saw you.'

Marion didn't know who his boss was, but imagined a big nasty biker.

'The gear is being flown in today,' he said. 'You'll have yours by tomorrow.'

Marion looked confused. 'What gear?'

The guy glanced around, like someone might be listening. 'Frazzle,' he whispered. 'You'll start off with two hundred pills for Stable Block. You can probably sell that in a couple of days.'

'I have no idea what you're talking about.'

'But you've spoken to your daddy?'

'About selling frazzle?' Marion asked furiously. 'No.'

'Sorry, I thought you were up to speed,' the weird biker said. 'Your old man found out who was smuggling for Mafia 13 and swapped frazzle for sweeteners. That's why everyone kicked off last night.'

'My dad?' Marion blurted. '*My* dad caused this?'

'Mafia 13 is getting wiped out,' the biker said enthusiastically. 'We have supply routes and bikers gonna be running drugs and everything else coming into this prison. Back the way it used to be.'

Marion's face was bright red. 'There was a fire in my cell block that could have killed me!' she spat. 'I spent ten hours kneeling in agony and two of my friends got smacked around for trying to use a drinking fountain.'

'Things kicked off more than anticipated,' the biker admitted. 'But your dad is basically a genius.'

'He's certainly something . . .' Marion said, sighing and shaking her head as she tried to keep calm and collect her thoughts. 'Tell your biker pals to hold off on sending me any frazzle for now. I need to make a phone call. Could you sneak me down to the mixing room before Kerry gets back?'

'Easy,' the biker agreed, as he flashed the swipe card around his neck. 'I can use this to take you down in the freight elevator.'

48. CAVALRY ARRIVES WITH BEANBAGS

While Diogo took *Dark Sky* out to refuel, Ollie flew drones and Cut-Throat went to meet a dealer who could supply his new drug empire with tens of thousands of frazzle pills, Robin spent the day crashed on his bunk in the houseboat.

It was good to be a slob sometimes. As Rage Cola tins and empty chocolate and crisp wrappers piled up around Robin, he read the latest gossip on his favourite hacking sites, watched trashy video clips and nodded off halfway through a yet-to-be-released superhero movie.

Robin finally got up and stumbled over to *Dark Sky* when Diogo told him he'd brought Indian food for dinner.

'We'll leave after we've eaten,' Diogo said, as he sat at *Dark Sky*'s galley table dabbing curry sauce on his naan. 'You looking forward to going back?'

'I don't know what's in these things, but they're delicious,' Robin said, as he bit a meat samosa before answering Diogo's question.

'Not looking forward to School Zone, sharing my room with Matt Maid, or seeing Josie and Alan play tonsil tennis. But my hacking guru D'Angela has sent over a bunch of puzzles that look interesting, my bed in the penthouse is super comfy, and even if it's mad living with Indio, Karma and all their kids, I kinda miss them.'

'I miss Napua,' Diogo said longingly. 'It'll be straight off to the bedroom for some lovin' when I get home.'

'Too much information!' Robin blurted, as he screwed up his face.

'Have you double-checked to make sure you haven't left anything behind on the houseboat?' Diogo asked.

Before Robin could answer, some loud swearing wafted across from Ollie's houseboat and there was a weird sound, like a champagne cork popping but *way* louder.

'AAAAAAAAARGGHHHH!' Cut-Throat roared. 'What are you doing?'

Diogo gave Robin a *what the heck* look and grabbed a pistol out of a drawer. As Robin snatched his bow and a couple of arrows, Diogo hopped onto the narrow ledge that ran around Ollie's houseboat and peeked through a window.

'You bloody shot me,' Cut-Throat shouted from inside the houseboat. 'Why did you bloody shoot me?'

When Robin stepped out of *Dark Sky*'s galley, he was stunned to see Josie standing on the shore, next to the enormous rebel known as Ten Man, because they said it took ten ordinary men to beat him in a fight.

'Hey, pal!' Josie said, as she gave a little wave.

Before Robin could ask what was going on, there was another loud pop.

'Stop shooting me, you lunatic!' Cut-Throat roared.

'This is only a beanbag gun, because I might need your help,' a woman shouted. 'I could happily stick you with real bullets after what you've pulled.'

It took Robin half a second to place the voice, which he usually heard screaming at kids over the penthouse dinner table.

Diogo looked at Robin as they both stepped onto the rear deck of the houseboat and peeked through a metal door into the living area.

Ollie sat on the floor with his hands up, Cut-Throat was sprawled over a broken coffee table groaning and holding his stomach, while his former wife Karma stood menacing them both with a giant riot control gun that was designed to flatten people by firing fist-sized beanbags.

'Put that thing down, we'll talk,' Cut-Throat pleaded. 'Whatever your problem is.'

'How can you not know what my problem is?' Karma gasped. 'Our thirteen-year-old daughter is in prison. She's having a tough time, but some part of your idiot brain has decided that the best way to help her is to turn her into a drug dealer!'

'All prisons have drugs,' Cut-Throat said. 'If we're not making that money, someone else is.'

'If you say one more word, my next beanbag might go somewhere more sensitive than your useless fat belly,' Karma shouted, as she lowered the gun. She'd spotted Robin and Diogo looking inside, and turned her fury on them. 'You two, get in here now.'

As Robin and Diogo walked inside sheepishly, Josie and Ten Man stepped onto the rear deck from the shore.

'I guess this shambles is what I should expect,' Karma sniped. 'From an idiot gang leader, two former bikers and a kid who ought to be in school.'

'Karma, I didn't know anything about drugs,' Robin complained. 'I came up here to help Marion.'

Robin flinched as Karma swung the beanbag gun in his direction.

'I warned you something would happen if you went with Cut-Throat,' Karma told Robin. 'Now sit all your asses down, shut your mouths and listen.'

49. DEFYING CONVENTIONAL WISDOM

As Robin and Diogo settled on a little couch, Josie and Ten Man entered the houseboat. Then Karma shot Cut-Throat in the gut with another beanbag.

'Stop it,' Cut-Throat begged, as tears welled in his eyes. 'I didn't even say anything.'

Karma leaned over Cut-Throat. 'That's for your daughter, who was in tears when she called me this morning. Marion was in a fire and two of her friends got beaten up by soldiers, because your idiot plan set off a riot. I'm normally a peaceful person, but this gun seemed like the only way I could express how angry you've made me, without actually killing you.'

Ten Man felt Karma was enjoying shooting her ex a little bit too much and coughed loudly. 'Shall we move on?' he suggested.

'I'll try,' Karma growled, as she leaned her oversized weapon against the hull of the boat. 'While you useless lot have been up here playing with drones and plotting to turn my thirteen-year-old into Pelican Island's number-one frazzle dealer, Josie used her brain and a fancy supercomputer to try and see if there was a way Marion could escape.'

'I looked,' Robin scoffed. 'Nobody has escaped from Pelican Island in eighty years.'

Josie stepped up close behind Robin and sounded knowledgeable. 'Pelican Island has a fearsome reputation, but since the prison was privatised and King Corporation took over, security has been slashed to the bone.

'I found photographs of Pelican Island from fifty years ago. The prison had its own patrol boats out on the lake twenty-four hours a day. There were huge searchlights and two guards in every watch tower. Nowadays, local teenagers cruise out to the island for a dare, ignore the warning buoys and spray graffiti on the cliffs.'

'She has a point,' Ollie said thoughtfully. 'We even found disposable barbecues on the shingles. Kids are having Pelican Island cook-outs and the guards let it slide.'

'They didn't when we went over there,' Robin pointed out.

'As far as I can work out, river police give kids a warning and escort them back across the lake,' Josie said. 'Robin and Ollie only got into a shootout because the cops would have recognised Robin and thrown him in jail.'

'So, you can get on the beach,' Robin said irritably. 'You still have to scale a forty-metre cliff and a massive perimeter wall with armed guards on top to get inside the prison.'

'Sure, Robin.' Josie sighed. 'I was just giving one example of how Pelican Island security isn't as tough as it used to be.

'I also found this website called HappyJobs, where adults post reviews about their employers. It has fifty-three reviews written by Pelican Island staff, and they all say the same stuff: broken intercoms and cameras, staff shortages, antiquated systems with file cards and rubber stamps. One guard posted that she quit her job because she was left on her own in charge of two hundred men, while the gate at the end of her cell block had rusted off its hinges.'

'That doesn't sound like an impregnable fortress,' Diogo noted.

Cut-Throat still held his beanbag-blasted gut, but had shuffled away from the flattened coffee table and propped himself against the side of the boat. 'Most successful jailbreaks are done by organised crime or terrorist groups,' he said. 'You need corrupt guards, and the ability to smuggle weapons and equipment.'

'We've got drones,' Ollie said.

'And Jay Patel,' Robin said. 'Though he might be in trouble if he gets blamed for switching the pills.'

Karma looked at Cut-Throat. 'Your biker monkey slaves might even be useful for once.'

'And Ten Man knows about this stuff,' Josie said.

Diogo, Ollie and Cut-Throat didn't know Ten Man, and they all looked at the big German rebel.

'I've robbed a few banks and close to a hundred jewellery stores,' Ten Man explained with a modest shrug. 'I know tunnels and explosives. I can crack most mechanical locks, including safes. In my younger days I had an unfortunate habit of partying hard, splashing my money around and getting caught. I escaped prisons in France, Romania and Canada.'

'Impressive,' Diogo admitted. 'But were any of those prisons on an island in the middle of a lake?'

Ten Man laughed. 'No, but I enjoy a challenge.'

Robin was thrilled by the idea of Marion getting out of prison, but still grumpy because he felt like Josie had outsmarted him. She'd used the Super with an open mind, while Robin had accepted the widely held belief that escaping Pelican Island was impossible.

'So, King Corporation is cheap and security isn't as good as it used to be,' Robin conceded, as he looked over his shoulder at Josie. 'But do you have a plan?'

'It won't be easy,' Karma said with a wry smile. 'We'll need Diogo's expertise with boats, Robin's sharp shooting, Cut-Throat's biker connections, Ten Man's escape experience and a healthy dollop of luck. There are details to iron out, but Josie and I have a plan and, with our combined skills, I think we can pull it off.'

'When?' Diogo asked.

'As soon as possible,' Karma said. 'There's a lot of nasty stuff on that island and I want my baby home before something bad happens.'

ELEVEN DAYS LATER

50. MONDAY TRAFFIC FANDANGO

Traffic going west on Route 172 peaked on Mondays, as families who'd spent weekends at their lake houses headed back to town for school and work.

Eleven-year-old Vince had caught the sun and his burnt skin itched as he sat wishing he could spend another day out sailing. He was in the back of his mum's Mercedes SUV, dressed in prep school uniform and frantically doing science homework.

'You were supposed to do that worksheet before we left,' Vince's dad was saying.

Vince's little sister had headphones on. His mum was frustrated with the traffic and scrolled through red congestion warnings on the dashboard nav screen.

'We should have left last night,' Vince's mum said, as the car ahead moved.

They rolled a few metres closer to a cable-stayed bridge over a tributary that fed into Lake Victoria.

'It's worse when the weather's fine,' Vince's mum told her husband. 'You may *just* make your train to Capital City, but the kids will be late for school.'

Vince was getting brain ache multiplying fractions, and looked up. The traffic going east towards the lake flowed freely, but a green TwoTu delivery van slowed to a stop as it neared the middle of the bridge.

'Do I see smoke from that truck?' Vince's dad asked, squinting into the early morning glare.

When the delivery van stopped, the smoke was obvious. Vince unbuckled and stood between the front seats for a better look.

'Darling, fasten your seat belt,' his mum said.

Vince ignored his mum as the smoke from under the van became more violent. Two people, who definitely weren't green-uniformed TwoTu workers, hopped out of the cab. One was a huge, bearded man, wearing the filthiest boots and jeans that Vince had ever seen. The other was almost as big, but clean-shaven and wearing a tracksuit.

'It might explode,' Vince said excitedly, as the pair from the van jogged off the bridge and along the empty eastbound lane towards him. 'I did a project on electric vehicles. If batteries get punctured, they overheat and . . .'

'Don't be silly, Vincent,' his dad interrupted, as the joggers passed the Mercedes, hurdled bushes and vanished down a roadside flood channel. 'Do what your mother told you and *sit down*.'

A three-metre orange jet blasted from the underside of the TwoTu van. The next explosion made ears pop and threw the delivery van sideways, scorching the road and melting plastic on cars trapped in the next lane.

As the van's flimsy cargo compartment burst open, Vince's sister squealed and grabbed his legs. A fireball shot fifteen metres in the air and the tilting van bounced off the thick metal cables holding the bridge up.

Vince noticed movement to his left. He glanced away from the flames as a powerful motorbike shot up the embankment, ridden by the two people from the van. The bike shrank to a dot as it accelerated to over a hundred kilometres per hour, tearing down the empty eastbound lane towards the lake.

It took three thousand batteries to power the delivery van, and Vince was reminded of microwave popcorn as each cell grew hot enough to burst with a loud pop and a whoosh of flame. Passengers on the bridge ran from damaged cars, while drivers tried U-turns as their vehicles got pelted with hot debris.

'This is so cool,' Vince blurted. 'My mates won't believe it!'

'Vincent, people are probably hurt,' his mum said firmly, then sighed. 'And they'll close the bridge. We'll be stuck here for *hours*.'

51. EVERYONE HATES THE COPIER

Ten kilometres east of the exploding van, Robin Hood sat on the balcony of a ritzy hotel room, eating room service bacon and eggs, with a view over the poshest part of Lake Victoria's waterfront.

Cut-Throat's voice came out of a walkie-talkie standing on an outdoor table. 'Me and Ollie made a nice explosion,' Cut-Throat said, as his motorbike roared in the background.

'Nice work, see you shortly,' Ten Man replied, as he walked onto the balcony and nicked one of Robin's bacon rashers.

'Hey!' Robin protested, though the breakfast was massive so it was no biggie.

Ten Man stepped up to the balcony railing and took in the view. There was a morning mist over the lake and if you didn't look too hard, Pelican Island could be mistaken for a castle.

But Ten Man's focus was a waterfront building a hundred metres from the balcony. It had four police vehicles out front. At the rear, a pier stretched into the lake, with two police launches and a high-speed rescue dinghy.

'Cops just found out about the explosion,' Ten Man told Robin, as officers ran from the police station building, fastening jackets and equipment belts.

Five cops bickered over who went in which car. As two vehicles sped west, sirens wailing, one officer ran back inside for a medical kit and threw it in the back of a pickup.

'That's five officers and three vehicles out,' Ten Man said, as Diogo joined them on the balcony and stole another of Robin's bacon rashers. 'I've had eyes on those cops for days and there's never more than six regular officers on duty.'

'Who does that leave?' Robin asked.

'The station commander, a receptionist and two river police.'

'No sign of boats leaving?' Diogo asked.

Ten Man shook his head. 'There's a weir between the lake and the bridge, so boats are useless.'

Diogo gave the back of Robin's chair a friendly kick. 'Time to stop stuffing your face and get ready.'

'Already ready,' Robin said. 'Except I need to pee because you were in the toilet for hours.'

Robin, Diogo and Ten Man wore dark clothes and carried backpacks full of equipment as they headed down six floors in the hotel elevator, then out onto the waterfront. The area in front of the hotel had lush lawns, yachts and restaurants, but at this time on a weekday the only people around were joggers and a guy driving a ride-on street sweeper.

They crossed the deserted waterfront road, entered the police parking lot, then split. Robin and Diogo went around the side of the police station towards the lake. Ten Man went through the main door and pressed the buzzer at a bulletproof reception counter.

He'd waited long enough to read a notice about burglary prevention and find Robin's picture atop the **Police Most Wanted** poster when an angsty young receptionist dashed up. Her name badge said Jo.

'Sorry to keep you,' Jo said. 'It's only my second week and they just called in a major incident.'

'No worries.' Ten Man smiled as he flashed an ID badge. 'I'm from OfficeServ. Here to fix the X570.'

'Oh, the copier,' Jo said. 'Thank goodness! That thing does whatever it wants. The officers say it's haunted.'

Jo opened a door to let Ten Man behind the counter.

There was no ghost in the photocopier, but Josie had found it was accessible from the station's public Wi-Fi network, then made it repeatedly crash by trying to print stuff on the wrong sized paper.

Outside, Diogo stood over a junction box on the station's side wall. Inside were neat racks of wires that brought phone, broadband and power into the building.

While Diogo waited, Robin squelched down the muddy embankment where land met water, then squatted in a cobwebbed space beneath the pier.

'I'm inside,' Ten Man whispered to his radio as Jo rushed off to answer a ringing phone. 'Are you ready?'

'Ready,' Diogo confirmed, pulling a black balaclava over his face.

'Just notched my arrow,' Robin agreed. 'Let's do this.'

52. FEEL LUCKY, PUNK?

While Ten Man stepped up to the X570 photocopier, unzipped a plastic tool case and pretended to know what he was doing, Robin bobbed out from beneath the pier and unleashed an arrow with a piece of plastic explosive no bigger than a pea.

His target was a waterproof connection box halfway up the police station's communication mast. It had aerials for the radios cops used on land, and a powerful maritime antenna enabling river police to communicate with boats across the entire lake.

The shot was easy from close range. As the box disintegrated with a bang loud enough to make windows rattle, Diogo opened the junction box on the ground and used a crowbar to rip out phone, broadband and power lines.

After firing his arrow, Robin sprinted to the rear of the police station and clambered up a gutter pipe to the building's flat roof.

There were several solar panels on the roof – and the police station's back-up battery. Robin pulled out a connecting wire that brought solar power into the building, then nervously used an electrical screwdriver to short out the terminals. If Ten Man was right, this would trip a fuse and kill the back-up power.

Directly below Robin's boots, Jo and the station's commanding officer had been plunged into gloom and confusion.

'Radios, phones gone and no back-up power,' the commander told Jo warily, as he marched across the open-plan office and opened a door to the boat crew's office. 'Have you guys got communications?'

Nobody looked Ten Man's way as he opened the reception door and let the masked Diogo inside. Then Ten Man pulled a large pistol out of his tool case and shot a bullet into a metal file cabinet to get everyone's attention.

'Everyone on the ground!' Ten Man said, loud but calm, as Jo gave an ear-splitting squeal. 'Nobody gets hurt if you do *exactly* what I say.'

One of the two river police officers stood in the office doorway and did what he was told, but the second sprinted out of a back door.

'Emergency, emergency. Does anyone copy?' the officer yelled into her radio as she ran onto the pier.

Her boots were noisy on the wood and she only made six steps before two arrows whipped past. The first was close enough to feel as it swooshed past her head, and the second shot in a high arc so that it speared the wooden pier in front of the fleeing officer.

'The next one won't be a warning shot,' Robin shouted, then made a dramatic jump off the roof and notched another arrow.

'Hood, you spotty little turd,' the cop snarled, as she stopped running and turned slowly to face him.

'Hands where I can see,' Robin ordered as the cop gave him psycho eyes.

'I can't wait to read the news when Guy Gisborne whips you raw.'

'Well, you're a sweetie pie,' Robin noted, as Diogo came outside to help. 'Walk back inside. No sudden moves.'

Back in the station, Ten Man had ordered his three hostages to throw down mobile phones and police radios. Then he made the commander unlock a small custody cell and step inside it.

The commander was followed into his own cell by Jo and the male river police officer. But the woman who'd run was a firecracker, throwing punches and spitting at Diogo when he took her radio. Robin found a high-vis vest and wrapped it around her head to stop the spitting, then helped Diogo drag her across the floor and cuff her to a heating pipe.

'You'll rot in jail, turd!' the officer screamed.

Ten Man's prisoners were better behaved and he rewarded them with bottled water and custard cream biscuits before slamming their cell door.

Out in the lobby, Diogo locked the station's main entrance and taped a handwritten notice to the glass:

We're sorry!
This police station is temporarily closed due to a power failure.
If your matter is urgent, please dial 999.

As Diogo attached the last piece of sticky tape, Cut-Throat and Ollie rolled into the parking lot on their motorbike.

'How's it going?' Ollie asked, dripping sweat.

Diogo let them in.

Cut-Throat eyed the last police car and pulled a big knife to slash its tyres.

'All good,' Diogo said. 'We had a runner but Robin handled her.'

Cut-Throat looked at Ollie and clapped his leather-gloved hands. 'Time to steal some police boats!'

53. DON'T MESS WITH CHRISSIE

Marion had barely finished her regular walk between Stable Block and the Arts and Crafts workshop when a message from Robin pinged on her phone.

In the boats.
On our way!

Marion gave Freya a discreet nod, made sure nobody was nearby, then messaged back.

See you soon
Hopefully :-)

Freya moved around the workshop, signalling to the escape party. Sophie took a bag of sticks from an art supplies cupboard and hurried to the bathroom. She was accompanied by a fourteen-year-old forest kid named Mila who was serving seven years for stealing a supermarket delivery van.

The escape party would also include two juvenile male inmates, fourteen-year-old Bukayo and Mila's sixteen-year-old brother, Uwe, while the last of the seven escapees, and the only adult, was Chrissie.

Chrissie had a minor career as a professional kickboxer, but was now doing fourteen years for fixing MMA bouts and scamming millions from bookmakers. She'd earned her place as an escapee because she was married to the leader of Brigands Motorcycle Club's powerful Capital City chapter. The plan also needed someone old enough to pass as a guard, and a pro fighter would be handy if things went wrong.

Marion's friend and cellmate Lola was staying behind because she had less than a year on her sentence left and would never get her baby back if she escaped. There were more than twenty other inmates spread around the Arts and Crafts space, so Marion couldn't put on a big show, but she gave Lola a quick hug and whispered, 'I used all the money on my blue card. There's chocolate, shampoo and soap tucked in your bed.'

Lola smiled and whispered back, 'Try not to get shot.'

'Visit me at Sherwood Castle,' Marion said, as tears welled up. 'I'd love to meet your son.'

'So would I,' Lola said sadly.

The other inmates would notice if seven people left the room at once. Marion checked that Jay Patel was in his usual position behind his desk, building Lego, then gave Chrissie a nod and started walking to the double-doored exit.

As Marion passed Freya and Bukayo, they were at a woodwork bench, unscrewing the legs from a pair of dining chairs they'd been making.

None of the other rooms in education block got used, so the guard always sat outside Arts and Crafts in a plastic bucket chair.

'No messing, ladies,' the guard said wearily as they stepped out. 'Whatever the excuse, you're going nowhere.'

Marion was shocked when Chrissie pounced. The guard was big, but Chrissie's kick sent him spinning off his chair, then she dived on top and put him in an eye-popping chokehold. The guard was unconscious in seconds and the move was so ruthless it reminded Marion of a documentary she'd seen where a giant python squashed a lamb.

'Open the classroom!' Chrissie said.

There was CCTV in the main hallway, but with hundreds of cameras on the island and a handful of busy staff in the control room, the chances of being noticed were slim. Chrissie dragged the guard into an empty classroom which had modern fixtures but dead air, like nobody had been inside for months.

While Chrissie pulled off the unconscious prison officer's shoes and uniform, Marion ran back to the Arts and Crafts room and gave Freya a *come on* signal. As

Freya exited with Bukayo, they carried the eight slender chair legs, which had now been bolted into pairs to make four wooden bows.

'They look sturdy,' Marion noted.

'My ma makes furniture,' Bukayo explained. 'She'd criticise my carpentry, but they'll do the job.'

Chrissie buttoned up a guard's blazer that was way too big, then put a dark wig over her buzz cut and slid on a pair of amber sunglasses. At the same time, Bukayo and Freya threaded their homemade weapons with lengths of Dacron bow string that had been smuggled in by drone.

Ollie's drones had also brought the escapees plastic arrow flights, ten regular arrowheads and four fitted with explosives. Sophie and Mila arrived in the classroom next, after spending five minutes in the women's toilets attaching flights and arrowheads to the wooden sticks.

The last escapee to leave Arts and Crafts was Mila's brother Uwe. The sixteen-year-old's nervy temperament and slight build made him a target for bullies, and one of them decided to follow him out.

'Where you sneaking off to, skinny boy?' a thug called Tim shouted as he entered the hallway. 'Want to kiss my shoe again?'

It was always likely someone would spot seven escapees, so Marion was ready for it.

'Wassup, lads?' Marion said, acting happy and drugged as Tim realised there was no guard in the hallway

'What you doing?' Tim demanded.

'Chill, bruv!' Marion said. 'Got some real gear to smoke, not frazzle!'

Tim looked doubtful, but the lure of a girl with drugs was strong. He cracked up laughing when he saw Chrissie in sunglasses and guard's uniform, but regretted it when she sent him crashing into school desks with a savage kick in the back.

'You're dead,' Tim roared, as he spun and punched.

Chrissie ducked, twisted Tim into an excruciatingly painful wrist lock and hissed in his ear. 'You're going to keep an eye on that guard for me,' she said, as Tim's knees buckled. 'If he comes around, you knock him out again. If you mess up, I'll tell my biker friends to cut your thumbs off.'

'You're mad trying to escape,' Tim growled. 'They'll slam you in punishment cells for so long you'll lose your minds.'

'Nobody asked for your opinion,' Chrissie snarled, as she let Tim go. 'Shut up and do what you're told.'

Marion checked the time on her miniature phone. 'Three minutes behind schedule,' she warned. 'We need to get moving.'

54. DEAD, DEAD, DEAD

'Moving six inmates,' Chrissie said, as she held the intercom button.

There was mighty relief when the education block's outer gate buzzed. Chrissie led the way into fresh air in her oversized guard uniform, tailed by Marion, Bukayo, Freya, Milo, Uwe and Sophie.

Marion didn't hesitate when Karma told her escape might be possible. But the reality felt terrifying now she was crossing the exercise yard in front of Stable Block, with nowhere to hide her bow and Chrissie in a guard's uniform that looked like fancy dress.

This time tomorrow she could be back at Sherwood Castle with everyone she loved. Or in the cruel white light of a punishment cell, covered in bruises and left for months with no human contact.

Put one foot in front of the other.
Try not to think about it.

But Marion was more scared than she'd ever been as

Chrissie tried to find the right key for the courtyard's exit gate. This led into a little wire cage and a second gate that had to be unlocked by a guard.

Just getting busted with a phone and weapon will add two years to my sentence.

Imagine the smug look on Danielle's face . . .

They waited two nerve-wracking minutes in the windswept cage before a floppy-haired guard called Nolan cruised up, twirling his key chain. He sometimes guarded the Arts and Crafts room, so he'd seen Chrissie in inmate clothes.

We're dead, we're dead, we're dead, Marion thought, as sweat drenched her faded orange shirt. There was so much dread on Sophie's face that Marion wanted to hold her hand.

'When did you start?' Nolan asked, as he eyed Chrissie's uniform.

Chrissie had learned all she could about guard training, and sounded more confident than Marion felt.

'Just finished in the training room,' Chrissie said. 'This is my second day in the wild. I'm supposed to be accompanied for two weeks, but they're short-staffed.'

'Arts and Crafts?' Nolan asked.

Chrissie nodded.

'Easy job to start, at least,' Nolan said as he unlocked the gate. 'Those inmates know they're on a cushy number, so there's never any trouble.'

'I've got to take this lot to Reception Room Five,' Chrissie said. 'I think it's straight through Central, then left?'

Nolan looked surprised. 'Reception Five? That's where the warden meets the high and mighty. All finger buffets and sparkling apple juice.'

'This lot are showing some committee their art projects,' Chrissie said, as the prisoners streamed through the gate.

'I heard Jay Patel gets paid fifty an hour,' Nolan said, shaking his head. 'Sits there building Lego and hasn't got a teaching qualification.'

Chrissie tutted. 'But they can't supply a uniform that fits me.'

'Once I pass my accountancy exams, I'm outta here,' Nolan said, as he closed the gate and started walking back to his post. 'Keep safe.'

'Hoping I'll be out of here before long too,' Chrissie joked once Nolan was out of earshot.

Marion felt too sick to laugh, but Freya and a couple of the others did.

Chrissie led the six down a mossy concrete slope and into one of the damp passageways that ran towards Central. Leaking waste pipes left the gloomy tunnels with a stomach-churning aroma, but on the upside, guards refused to work in the stench. They eased through three sets of double gates with one key and a buzz to the prison control room.

Marion's nerves hit a new peak when they reached Central's busy hexagonal atrium, with the noise from ten floors of male prisoners above. One shackled inmate recognised Chrissie in her guard's uniform, doing a double take but keeping her mouth shut.

The air grew fresher as Chrissie reached a freshly painted gate with an old-fashioned varnished wooden sign overhead:

Special Visitors, Reception Rooms,
Wedding Chapel & Wardens' Offices

Beyond the bars were chequered black and white tiles, a hexagonal reception counter and a curved staircase that would have been at home in a grand country house. This part of the prison could only be accessed by appointment, and even Chrissie seemed anxious as her thumb squeezed a doorbell.

55. THE POSH BIT

'There are no inmates on today's list,' said the snooty guard, peering through the black gate. She looked like she put on make-up with a trowel and her stacked-up hairdo and dangly earrings definitely wouldn't be practical if an inmate kicked off.

As Freya stepped up to the gate, Marion glanced about, aware of staff crossing the atrium who might realise Chrissie wasn't one of them, or notice that their art objects were bows and arrows.

'Officer, you need to listen very carefully,' Freya whispered. 'Your name is Joan Frick. You live at 73 Borstal Road with your husband John. But we've seen your social media and we know that the real loves of your life are your cats, Mabel, Tilly and Belle. You're scared, because you haven't seen the cats for a couple of days, but let me assure you, my biker friends are taking good care of them.'

'For now,' Sophie added menacingly.

Freya paused while Joan Frick gasped. Marion didn't like the idea that the escape plan involved Brigands kidnapping cats, or that her future relied on Joan Frick risking her job to save them.

'If you want to see your kitty-cats again you will open this gate,' Freya continued. 'Then you'll escort us to reception and give us the electronic key card to access Reception Room Five.'

'Miaow!' Sophie added mockingly, as she made little cat claws with her hands.

Marion felt sure Joan Frick would run back to her desk and pull the emergency alarm. The Central SWAT team was stationed across the hexagonal lobby. They'd be on the escapees within seconds, and they had a reputation as the most brutal squad on the island.

'If one hair is harmed on my cats, I'll hunt all of you down,' Joan Frick warned, as she entered a PIN to open the inner gate.

Frick looked shaky and tearful as she walked behind the grand reception desk and took a white swipe card out of a drawer.

'I love cats,' Freya told the guard reassuringly, as Chrissie led the way towards the stairs. 'They'll be fine if you keep your mouth shut.'

Marion felt like she'd landed on another planet as she headed up the curved staircase and along a hallway. There was carpet under her feet, black-and-white pictures of past wardens on wallpapered walls, radiators that actually produced heat, and a whiff of cleaning spray instead of armpits and sewage.

At the top of the stairs the prison's senior staff offices branched off in one direction, while the reception rooms went the other. Weddings were only allowed for pregnant or terminally sick inmates, so the escapees were surprised to see a small, but noisy, gathering as they marched swiftly past the wedding chapel.

Reception Room Five was through a large door at the furthest end of the hallway. Chrissie tapped the white key card on the lock and smiled with relief as it clicked open.

The room was big enough to seat fifty, with a stage at one end. Presently the space was set up for staff training, with grouped tables and display boards showing lists of rules on prisoners' rights.

'They've got biscuits!' Mila said, as she grabbed a pink wafer from a plate and was followed by grasping hands from her brother and most of the others.

'Are you OK?' Freya asked as she stepped up to Marion. 'You look pale.'

'I've never had nerves this bad,' Marion admitted, as Freya bit a hazelnut cookie.

The space's lurid orange-and-brown carpet gave it a 1970s vibe and Marion studied the view out of huge, unbarred windows set in hammered concrete. There was an expanse of flat roof over the island's machine shop. This obscured most of the loading dock beyond it, but

Marion could see bits of lake and navigation lights on the mast of a refuse barge.

'Two hundred metres from freedom,' Freya said hopefully. 'Help me roll the explosives.'

Freya took a squashy clingfilm-wrapped package of plastic explosive from one pocket of her shorts. After unwrapping, she halved it and gave one part to Marion.

'Roll it into one long sausage,' Freya instructed. 'It's not dangerous until I plug in the detonators.'

Marion leaned over a table and rolled the explosive on the flat surface as Bukayo gave a loud yelp. He'd been about to sit on the stage and eat a ginger nut when he saw a face peek out from the stage curtains.

Now he'd been spotted, the guard decided his best tactic was to spring for the door.

'Chrissie Strawberry!' the guard shouted, reaching for his stun gun as he hurdled off the stage and skipped Bukayo's attempt to grab his foot.

'Dead man!' Chrissie roared, as she tackled the guard, snatched the dangerous end of his stun stick and smashed him in the cheek with her fist. The guard's head thumped a table as he fell, and Chrissie's prison-issue boot as he hit the ground

'This dirtbag punched a seventy-year-old inmate because she didn't walk fast enough,' Chrissie explained, as she wrapped her arm around the guard's neck and choked him out. 'Smashed her nose, pinned the blame on me and got ten months added to my sentence.'

Chrissie rolled the guard onto his back and ripped open his jacket to see if he had pepper spray or anything else worth stealing. A red light flashed on the radio clipped to his belt.

'Trouble!' Chrissie blurted. 'Guard pushed his emergency alarm.'

'That button leaves the microphone open on the emergency channel,' Mila warned. 'The control room can hear every word we say.'

'Hate this guy so much!' Chrissie said, as she ripped the radio off the guard's belt and unclipped the battery pack.

'Now what?' Mila asked.

'No change,' Chrissie said.

'No way back from here,' Freya agreed, as she took charge. 'Sophie and I will set the explosives. Marion, you need to make a phone call. Tell Karma that the alarm will go off any second and we need those police boats at the loading dock now. The rest of you, wedge every piece of furniture against the door. SWAT will be here any second.'

56. PROJECT MAXIMUM CONFUSION

Ollie and Cut-Throat had boarded one police launch, while Diogo took the other. As the pair headed towards Pelican Island's loading dock, Robin and Ten Man raced ahead in the orange rescue dinghy.

A kilometre from the lakefront, Robin's boat liaised with a black RIB, with Ísbjörg, Karma and Josie on board. Ísbjörg passed Robin a handheld rocket launcher, some extra explosive arrows and a nylon holdall filled with clanking smoke grenades.

'Gonna be quite the party,' Robin joked, but nobody laughed.

As the two fast RIBs blasted towards Pelican Island, the slower police launches dropped further behind.

Josie and Karma cut their engines a few hundred metres from the island's eastern tip, while Robin and Ten Man powered on through the line of warning buoys. They sped past graffitied limestone cliffs and shingle beaches, reasonably confident that guards wouldn't shoot a boat with police markings.

A hundred metres shy of the island's loading dock and close to the meat warehouse where Marion did her punishment shifts, Ten Man steered the police rescue boat behind a breakwater, built to keep the island's current away from the loading dock.

As Robin scrambled clumsily over boulders and bulldozed chunks of old prison buildings, Ten Man dragged the rescue boat out of the water and tipped it against the cliff face so that guards up on the wall couldn't see.

Robin unhooked his radio and was planning to tell Diogo they'd arrived when a siren erupted across the whole island. As Robin glanced warily up the prison wall towards a guard tower, he wondered if he'd caused the alarm.

Diogo spoke over the radio, but the siren drowned him out.

'Repeat, please,' Robin told his radio, then held the speaker to his ear.

'The escapees are in the reception room. They've set the explosives around the window, but there's a SWAT team on their backs.'

'Roger that,' Robin said, as he gave Ten Man a thumbs up.

Ten Man picked up the rocket launcher and aimed it towards a metal tower atop a small building on the far side of the loading dock. His aim was poor, but the projectile packed enough explosive to rip out five metres of prison wall and send Pelican Island's main communication tower crashing into the lake.

As Robin shielded his face from billowing dust, Josie was on the black RIB launching three T8 drones carrying sticks of mining explosive.

Robin had pre-programmed their flight paths. If things went to plan, the first drone would damage the chopper and helipad on Central's roof, while the second would take out a substation that controlled Pelican Island's electricity supply.

The final drone carried three sticks of explosive and would deliver a huge explosion to an abandoned guard post on the far side of the island. Hopefully this would distract some prison staff from the loading dock.

When the dust had mostly cleared, Robin took binoculars from his pack, propped himself behind a boulder and studied the loading dock and the back of the meat warehouse.

'How's it look?' Ten Man asked.

A trash barge and a vessel with three refrigerated meat containers obstructed Robin's view, but the part of the dock he could see had six prisoners who'd followed the rules and lain down when the alarm sounded.

A group of white-coated warehouse supervisors stared nervously at the explosion site and there were three guards. Two stood on the dockside, guarding prisoners with stun sticks drawn. The third officer perched in the lookout on the warehouse roof with a rifle.

'Marion and her pals have to run across the machine shop roof and straight towards the guard with the rifle,' Robin shouted over the siren. 'I'll have to take her out.'

'Wait for the explosion,' Ten Man shouted back as he unzipped the holdall filled with smoke grenades.

Robin tried not to think about the guard on the roof as he slid his bow from his backpack and wiped drips of lake water on a rag. It was never easy to shoot a person, but it was a hundred times worse if you had time to look at them and wonder if they had kids, or what they watched on TV.

As Robin looked at two police launches plough between warning buoys and close rapidly on the landing dock, explosions came in succession. First on the roof of Central with a satisfying fireball of aviation fuel. Two more drones exploded on the far side of the island, and seconds later a small blast sent a tremor rippling across the machine shop's metal roof.

'That's got to be the reception room,' Ten Man shouted, as he grabbed a smoke grenade out of the nylon bag. 'We should see the escapees in a few seconds.'

57. OUT OF IDEAS FOR CHAPTER TITLES

Thousands of windows on Pelican Island had rusting metal bars, but the reception rooms had bulletproof glass.

Freya had moulded worms of plastic explosive into the upper corners of one huge square window. Marion tried to stop her fingers shaking as she helped her cousin wire the fuses, but the SWAT team trying to smash their way in didn't help.

'Come on!' Sophie urged pointlessly, as Marion dived onto the stage with the other escapees and buried her head.

'Open your mouths,' Freya warned, trailing a strand of fuse wire as she backed away from the glass. 'If you don't, the shockwave will burst your ear drums.'

It is a very bad idea to stay in a room when half a kilo of plastic explosive is set off, but the seven escapees had no choice.

Freya completed the detonation circuit by touching two wires to a nine-volt battery.

Marion screamed as the blast sent an incredible searing pain through her head. The heat blistered the skin on her arms and left her ears ringing.

The stage curtains were ablaze, the nylon carpet had turned to toffee and half the ceiling had come down, but as the dust cleared it seemed the huge bulletproof window hadn't budged a millimetre.

'Are you bloody kidding me!' Freya screamed, as she inhaled the swirling dust.

The SWAT team had smashed through the desks wedged against the door, but Chrissie wasn't giving up.

'I'd rather die than get caught!' she roared, as she charged with the stun stick she'd taken from the unconscious guard.

She ripped the helmet off the first guy who tried to clamber over tangled chairs and tables, then nipped his bald dome with fifty thousand volts. The leader of the SWAT team decided to change tactics.

'They might have guns,' he shouted. 'We'll throw in gas till their eyes bleed.'

Freya pounded furiously on the bulletproof window.

It was an act of frustration, but the huge slab of glass shifted. It hadn't shattered or dropped out as planned, but heat from the blast had melted the sealant that held the glass in its frame.

'Help me push!' Freya screamed, as a hissing can of tear gas clattered through the tangled furniture and landed close to her feet.

Nobody heard with the smoke, ringing ears and prison siren still blasting. Freya had to gesticulate wildly and drag Marion and Bukayo off the stage.

'Push, push!' Freya urged, with added gestures.

The tear gas was getting thick, burning eyes and throats as Freya ploughed her shoulder against the window. When Marion, Bukayo and Mila joined the effort the bulletproof glass began to tilt.

'One more!' Freya pleaded, as the SWAT team charged into the room.

As Uwe shot a SWAT officer with an arrow and Chrissie kneed another in the face, eight hundred kilos of bulletproof glass toppled from its frame and smashed a hole through the machine shop's metal roof.

While shocked inmates glanced up from sewing machines and cutting tables, Marion led the escapees with a two-footed leap from the window ledge.

After barely clearing the giant hole in the roof, Marion began a sprint across the corrugated metal towards the loading dock. Ten Man had been firing smoke grenades since he heard the explosion at the window, so within twenty metres Marion was shrouded in grey.

Chrissie was last out of Reception Room Five, but only after throwing a SWAT officer through the hole in the machine shop's roof. Once Chrissie was clear, Freya and Uwe used their homemade bows and shot explosive-tipped arrows through the missing window.

As the SWAT officers in the reception room screamed, panicked and rolled around to put out their flaming clothes, the seven inmates sped across the machine shop roof, hidden by Ten Man's barrage of smoke grenades.

Marion was first to reach the lookout at the roof's edge. The guard was unconscious, with Robin's favourite brand of carbon-fibre arrow speared through her chest. It was a gory sight, but after all the misery the guards had inflicted, she felt zero sympathy.

58. SPECIAL HAIR MOMENTS

Marion's eyes streamed from tear gas and she was still practically deaf from the explosion, but she had the brains to pick up the guard's rifle before setting off down a rusty spiral staircase to the dock.

The scene on the waterfront had turned manic. Inmates had overpowered guards and knocked them out or thrown them in the water. Smoke was everywhere and Robin added to the confusion by blowing random stuff up.

One explosive arrow had destroyed two wooden props, leaving guards trapped in a watchtower that dangled precariously over the prison wall. Another had started a huge fire in the trash barge.

The two police launches hadn't been fired on by guards as they approached the dock, but had confused inmates, who thought they were real cops. Several inmates threw stuff at the boats as they tried to dock.

A group of bikers stormed over to protect the police boats, then started fighting among themselves. Cut-Throat had arranged for eight bikers to get put on punishment duty in the meat warehouse and join the escape, though only after Karma had checked their criminal records to ensure they weren't freeing a bunch of murderous lunatics.

Fist fights broke out when bikers who'd used the chaos to escape jobs in trash disposal decided to have a go at boarding the police boats. Ollie was forced to fire warning shots over their heads and two bikers ended up in the water.

As Marion stepped off the stairs and ran along the dockside towards the police launches, she glanced into the warehouse where she'd spent so many torturous hours. Inmates were going berserk, standing on high shelves hurling boxes, setting off fire extinguishers and smashing equipment.

Freya ran behind Marion and almost got run over by a speeding forklift with two madmen hanging off the back. The madmen jumped clear, but forklift and driver shot off the end of the dock and crashed into the water.

Eight passengers and two crew was plenty for each little police launch, especially when most of them were hundred-kilo bikers. Marion felt like a little girl as she grasped her daddy's giant tattooed hand and got lifted aboard.

'Sweetheart!' Cut-Throat said, giving Marion a quick kiss, then waving Freya and the others on towards Diogo's boat.

'Too many fat bikers!' he shouted. 'We'll bloody sink!'

Marion's eyes were ablaze from the tear gas, but she knew anyone left behind would be treated brutally, so she watched carefully as Freya, Chrissie, Bukayo, Mila and Uwe boarded Diogo's boat.

Sophie had sliced her leg on the metal roof when she'd jumped out of the reception room and left a trail of bloody shoeprints as she boarded last.

'That's everyone,' Marion told her dad, as about twenty SWAT officers charged around the far end of the loading dock.

They looked fearsome as they drummed stun sticks on their riot shields, but scattered when two prisoners drove at them in forklifts. Inmates who'd climbed onto the machine shop roof pelted the SWAT officers with strips of guttering and wire mesh as they tried to escape, while one of Robin's arrows exploded in the cab of a dock crane over their heads.

As Cut-Throat put the rudder hard over and opened the boat's throttle, a woman dived into the overloaded boat, only to be chucked in the water by snarling bikers. The police launch was low in the water with so many bodies, but that didn't stop cheers erupting, as the bikers hugged each other and gave Ollie and Cut-Throat manly thumps on the back.

'Life without parole, kiss my arse!' a biker standing at the back of the boat shouted, and flipped off Central tower.

Diogo steered his boat out seconds behind Cut-Throat. He took a course closer to the burning trash barge and felt heat from the flames as Chrissie gave him a soggy kiss.

'Where's the beer?' she asked.

Diogo laughed as he studied his radar, then spoke into his radio. 'I see no drones, no boats, no helicopters. I'd say the plan to block roads and take out communications has worked a treat.'

Karma's voice came back through the speaker. 'We've just reached south shore. Ten dirt bikes are fuelled and ready for the forest.'

While the police launches were sluggish with so many escapees on board, Robin's rescue boat remained blazing fast. Ten Man let him drive as they blasted away from the weary prison siren and smoke plumes over Pelican Island.

Robin bounced the orange dinghy over the wash from the police launches, then cruised up alongside Cut-Throat's launch. Although they'd been in a prison that didn't allow TV or internet, most of the escaped bikers knew who Robin was and waved or shook fists at him.

'You the man, Robin!' one jubilant biker shouted.

But it was Marion Robin was desperate to see. He found himself sobbing as she pushed between the bikers and waved from the side of the boat.

'How's your day been?' Robin shouted, as tears streaked his face.

Instead of answering, Marion jumped in the lake.

'Bloody hell!' Robin gasped as he cut the throttle and circled back towards her.

Marion was usually the sensible one, but the torment of being locked up had messed with her head and she had to do something wild to feel that she was really free.

'We'll get her, keep going,' Ten Man told the two police launches over his radio as he took the controls from Robin.

Marion was an excellent swimmer. As Robin fished her out of the water, her eyes were bright red from tear gas, she had small burns from the window explosion and she smelled of smoke, but bliss pulsed through Robin as he decided that Marion in a soggy prison uniform was the most beautiful thing he'd ever seen.

Marion shivered and laughed as Ten Man opened the throttle to catch the other vessels. She crawled up next to Robin in the floor of the boat and kissed him quickly on the lips, then playfully flicked his ear.

'That's for leaving me behind in Locksley,' she said.

'Deserved,' Robin admitted.

'And you're crying,' Marion teased, as she rubbed her ear and realised that the ringing was mostly gone. 'You missed me!'

Robin's felt a childish urge to deny it, but he wasn't a kid any more. He slid his arm around Marion's back and squeezed her tight.

'Of course I missed you,' Robin sniffed, as the wind blasting over the speeding boat made their hair fly in a thousand directions.

Look out for more

ROBIN HOOD

ADVENTURES

Robert Muchamore's ROBIN HOOD series

Look out for

More ROBIN HOOD adventures to come!

Coming soon!

ROBIN HOOD

BALLOTS, BOMBS & BETRAYAL

It's election day and Robin Hood is using every trick
he knows to help get his dad elected as Sheriff of
Nottingham. But his rival Guy Gisborne not only
has the police in his pocket, but won't hesitate
to stuff ballot boxes with fake votes.

Meanwhile Robin's half-brother Little John is caught
up in his mother's presidential election campaign.
What will he do if both parents win?

The stakes have never been higher for both brothers
in the eighth book of this all-action series.

Robert Muchamore's books have sold 15 million copies in over 30 countries, been translated into 24 languages and been number-one bestsellers in eight countries including the UK, France, Germany, Australia and New Zealand.

Find out more at
muchamore.com

Follow Robert
on Facebook and Twitter
@RobertMuchamore

Thank you for choosing a Hot Key book.

If you want to know more about our authors
and what we publish, you can find us online.

You can start at our website
bonnierbooks.co.uk/HotKeyBooks

And you can also find us on:

We hope to see you soon!